ALL THAT TIME ALLOWS

I0556367

by

John Behardien

Duncurin
Publishing

Duncurin.com

First Published in England MMXVIII

Duncurin Publishing
Monton
England

Duncurin.com

ISBN : 978-0-9935169-8-6

Book Design : Moosey

DEDICATION

For my dear friends, Karl and Meriel.
Constantly missed. Forever in our thoughts. Sweet Dreams.

And for Robin my 'oldest' friend. Happy 'special' Birthday
and may you have many Happy and Healthy Returns.
With love.

WITH THANKS

My sincere thanks to the following very talented people:

Patrick Fahy: for his painstaking Copy/Edit skills. patfahy@lineone.net

Cover Photo: Courtesy of iStockPhoto: 'Grandriver' and 'Nesser3321'

Other Books By John Behardien

Crack In the Code
Stars' End

The Last Great Gift

Dawn Over Vancouver
All That Time Allows

Final Horizon
Final Request
Final Truth

One Life Many Moments

CONTENTS

CHAPTER I

Perfection In Death

She hesitated just outside the plywood-panelled door, recognising that it represented a far greater obstacle than its flimsy construction would have indicated. She took a breath, deep enough to make her feel even dizzier but, sadly, it didn't provide sufficient courage for the task she faced. She knew only, in those final seconds now closing mercilessly upon her, that she would have to compose herself if she were to stand a chance of getting through all the things that were brimming with urgency in her overwrought mind. Her shaking hands and quivering legs also gave their verdict on the distressing task that lay beyond that dark-stained and insubstantial door.

She detected, presciently, that the agony that was welling up within would defeat her even as he shouted in response to the quiet knock.

"Come in".

She tried to slow down her walking, but this only made her look more nervous and hesitant. Then she sped up and this made her look as if she almost stumbled on to the chair that he'd gestured towards. Sitting on the chair that he'd offered, she hoped that by straightening her back, as she used to do at school, she would, even then, defeat the tears that she couldn't quite control. However, even before that thought had expired within her consciousness, they started welling up from the corners of her glassy, brown eyes that were rapidly losing all traces of composure.

She felt as if her heart had stopped. For more than a moment she wished that it *would* stop and then at least she'd embrace oblivion, not this torment. It assured her, however, that not only was it still beating but was, in effect, doing its best to keep up with the flush of blood rampaging through her pretty head like an express train about to leave the rails.

Mercifully, he spoke first, thus giving her a few more seconds to fight down the stinging that was now tormenting her in both eyes. She blinked quickly in an attempt to subdue those tear glands that were making determined progress in stopping her from saying all that she had to say: for she knew that this was her very last opportunity to do so. She gasped repeatedly, hoping that he wouldn't notice, in an attempt to calm the quakes still issuing from her heart: all to no avail.

"Tina, my dear, what can I do for you?"

He was always so nice. This, by definition, was at the core of her problem. How much easier her task would be if he'd been a horrible person. Indeed, if he'd espoused such attributes, she'd have been on her way long ago. There would have been no point in staying for someone that she didn't like. Moreover, she'd never have felt the things that, she realised, she should have told him a long time ago.

The first tear tipped over the edge of her lower eye-lid. It was to be followed by many more as they fell into the abyss of misery. Tina knew, in that moment, that they would master her. More importantly, she'd be lucky to get through a fraction of the things she needed to tell him; and the last thing, the most vital one, that she just had to declare before her very heart burst with the anguish and pain that it had suffered for more months than she could contemplate.

"I've come to tell you that I am leaving." Although his mouth moved to form concern, she knew that she couldn't wait for him to speak for, if she did, she knew that her words would never restart. Her tears queued steadily, waiting for their opportunity to obliterate her. A moment's pause would free them.

"I can't stay, Dr Binder, she's hurt me for the very last time. She is such a manipulative, cruel woman. She's finally got her wish. I am leaving." Sad eyes looked away from him, she could voice no more.

To his credit, Neil Binder made no pretence at not knowing to whom his senior receptionist was referring.

"Come on now, she's not *that* bad, Tina. Are you sure we can't work something out?"

Her beset shiny, brown eyes met his at their deepest meditative shade, like two conkers waiting to be discovered by some eager little boy on a sunny autumnal afternoon. However, his eyes, far from reflecting the excitement that such unearthing would suggest, were of a much more gloomy hue that hung about him habitually; like a cloud that clung persistently to a beautiful mountain peak that even the sun couldn't get past. Even his words seemed flat and dejected. In point of fact, it was only concern for her and her obvious distress that had banished, fleetingly, the misery that was etched to his own face, it having become set in such a pose years before.

"No, Dr Binder, she's insulted me for the very last time. I am here to hand in my notice. She tells me that there has been a leak made to the local paper. Our casualty attendance rates have been divulged. Our *confidential* casualty attendance rates have been leaked. Ms Makepeace is implying that I am the only person in the whole surgery with the expertise, apart from her of course, Dr Binder, to extract such information from the computer system. I told her that I think it's her; that *she's* the one who's done it. What's more, I think she did this deliberately. More importantly, I think she did it for no other reason than to accuse me."

His dejected air was displaced only for the shortest interval of time as his handsome face creased into a fleeting smile, that itself was a rare thing to behold. Within seconds, however, the perennial cloak of sadness returned as he formed words. "Now, I know that you don't like Amanda, but she would not do that. She wouldn't *deliberately* leak such sensitive information to the press about our casualty attendance rates. We are in enough hot water as it is from the Clinical Commissioning Group about all our patients who queue up to be seen in Rivington General, Accident and Emergency. So, I can't believe that she would do that. Why would she do such a thing? Why would *anyone* do such a thing and then try to pin it on another? There must be some mistake, some other explanation. Surely she, like all of you, is someone who works so hard to keep us out of the bad books at the CCG."

Tina's outrage fuelled just enough strength for her to continue to voice some of the sentiments that were now queuing with urgency within. For the time being such thoughts served to grant the shortest of reprieves from her tears.

"You don't know her, Dr Binder; she's as nice as strawberry mousse to your face, but as hard as deep-frozen icicles when your back is turned." Her hands made a claw shape like a little girl at a party mimicking a lion. It lasted but a moment, like his smile. "At least, when *your* back is turned, with lots of sharp and nasty shards below the surface. You haven't seen what she gets up to when you aren't looking; when you're in here seeing to poorly folk and the staff and patients fall under her mercy."

He nodded but couldn't really picture the imagery his senior receptionist had presented.

Using the pause that had formed, she continued. "Well, let's put it this way, there are only two of us who are capable of extracting such detailed and powerful reports from the computer: and I can *assure* you it wasn't me. That information can only have come from this surgery. There's no other way, and it's been leaked: and leaked to cause mischief. You've made a pact with the devil; one who appears as a woman."

"As I said, there must be some mistake, Tina. She's not capable of doing that, and besides, you know we need her for the submission to the CCG next month."

Tina knew very well what was about to befall the quiet surgery with its wonderful, kind and talented senior partner – albeit the GP who'd drifted for some five years, this being the time that she'd known him. Ultimately, it looked as if in the eleventh hour, he'd continue to drift. He knew, as did everyone else, that the sharp rocks that lay ahead would be more than capable of capsizing his tiny, frail boat that continued to bring him directly on to that ragged unforgiving shore.

He had pinned his hopes on the practice manager who, Tina was convinced, was a false and duplicitous ally. She remained constant in the view that the manager's plans were strangers to the words; 'truthfulness', 'fair dealing' and 'loyalty'. She'd hoped, somehow, that impending disaster would, even now, wake him from his torpor. If only that would happen and his re-awakening would cause him to rush to the wheel, barking vital orders at his loyal crew; thereby saving his ship, and them, from certain doom. She pictured him momentarily in a partially ripped shirt, itself lashed by the wind, rain and sea spray as his arms, complete with rippling muscles, stretched out decisively to re-exert control. It was not to be.

The CCG was a group of local GPs and others that had been set up to administer and police services and standards provided by GPs. Such organisations existed up and down the land. Locally, however, everyone knew that they were now circling the small surgery like wolves following a limping donkey.

"It wasn't me, Dr Binder, and she and I are the only pair who could have generated that report to *leak* that information. I swear on my mother's life it wasn't me."

Even as the sentence escaped from her lips, at the speed of sound, she knew that her words were the wrong ones. Words which would do more harm than good, by a considerable margin. Ones that would inevitably remind him of something she'd hoped was firmly in the past. Deep within, she knew better. Moreover, she knew in that moment that she'd failed; the manager had won. Playing a risky strategy had not only banished victory but also assured Tina's departure. How she wished there and then that she could take back those words; but it could not be. It seemed as if in that second she, too, was condemned to look at the picture on his desk which had been, for five years' since, a mother's shrine.

Catching the slight glance, he did his best to generate a smile, despite seeing in that moment the sadness and regrets that flooded her face. Such a thing was now beyond him. He couldn't know, nor did he guess, that they had just swept away the words that she was then hoping to say. Nor could he help but revert to type and mirror her desolate looks. At least the depth of her regrets had caused a suspension of the tears that still moistened her eyes. Even the discomfort coming from her heart as it almost leapt from her chest paled beside the unremitting misery that now claimed her.

She gasped again and again desperately, but futilely, trying to over swallow air to make herself calmer but as a result, she only experienced more dizziness. Finally, she attempted a desperate strategy. One that she recognised as being bankrupt even as it formed on her lips, nevertheless that she felt she owed him before the events that her instinct told her would claim not only him but also all others at the little surgery.

"I'm the last one, Dr Binder, who can stop her." Although her words were calmer, her feelings inside remained in violent turmoil. She wanted to grip him by both his arms while she made him listen to all she had to say, and to acknowledge the danger he was in. More than this, most of all, she wanted to tell him something of her own feelings for him, and that these were ones that, she knew, like his grief, would never die.

"Now, Tina, she isn't that bad. Besides, I need her if we are to survive the CCG inspection to do with our casualty attendances and non-elective admissions."

Having come so far she realised she had nothing else to lose. Without doubt, she had already lost absolutely everything and that included him. And now he'd never know.

"You can't *trust* her Dr Binder, she will *destroy* this surgery and you, if need be. There must be something else, something she's telling nobody; somehow it's to do with you and this surgery and that's the *only* reason she's here. You, or somebody here, has something she wants and, once she's got it, she will show her true colours. *Think,*" she said, with more force than politeness would have sanctioned, "what is someone like her doing here amongst us – *she* doesn't belong here, surely we can all see that! She couldn't be further removed from her own name. *Make peace* is the last thing on her mind; it's like a cruel joke."

She realised in that fragment of time, when all that remained were cold and sterile ashes at her feet, that time and opportunity had long since passed into the realms of what might have been.

"Don't be so hard on her, Tina; perhaps you have not seen her qualities?"

Without doubt, this went to the heart of her problem: she'd seen how secretive, how duplicitous the manager could be; one who, Tina knew, would help herself first and who'd place everyone, and the surgery, a distant second. Without doubt, this applied also to helping the surgery to withstand the inspection that was coming their way, a review which threatened to obliterate them.

"I need her, Tina. The surgery needs her. She's our only hope," he could only offer the limited words by way of crumbs of consolation.

"I know that, Dr Binder," she acknowledged as she nodded sadly, "but you understand, don't you, that I can't stay. I can't forgive her for saying those things to me when she knows, when you know, how much I'd do for you."

Here it was, her opportunity to reveal something of her deeper thoughts. The secrets she'd done her best to conceal, until today, when it no longer mattered – how she felt about the kindest, most gentle man she had ever set eyes on.

Wanting to tell him that she'd stayed just for him, because she couldn't bear the thought of this kind, caring soul being at the mercy of a woman who was a study in cruelty. Even more than that, she wanted him to know how she *felt* about *him*. She even managed the intake of breath that would fuel those words. He'd stopped speaking, silence opened: his deep brown eyes studying her.

Had she continued to look directly into those eyes, she might have formed the words that she'd been rehearsing for months: no, for years. In glancing away her eyes couldn't help but fall on to the ring on his left hand and, once again, the little picture on his desk of the mother who still cradled the little boy, not two years old, as they slumbered forever in the local cemetery.

Such thoughts, though fleeting, were, nevertheless, enough to vanquish her. She bowed her head, now occupied with more sadness than even her tears could frame. Ultimately, she knew that you could not defeat a memory, for it was surely a thing of perfection. Nor could one defeat a love that would never die. And no one could compete with a woman who remained as perfect now, albeit in someone's memory, as the day she died. Tina understood, in that second, that they were not alone; that they had never been alone in the five years that had passed since that tragic day. For such memories came as close to perfection as made no difference; immaculate and unassailable in the minds of men. Nor could pure, deep and genuine love conquer all – as was widely held. And nobody could displace a dead woman; no matter how much the loneliness of two people demanded that it be so.

Other words appeared. Words of a woman resigned to defeat.

"I'll be leaving, then, in that case, Dr Binder."

"Is there some other way, Tina?"

"No, I realise things here will never change, and I should have gone ages ago. In truth, Dr Binder, I only stayed for you." The lengthiest of pauses appeared at this point as her eyes widened, her heart leapt in her chest, demanding that she say the words: but bravery had long since deserted her, and in that moment only sorrow remained. "Please, please be careful, Dr Binder, you don't know what she is capable of and what she does behind your back."

Tina knew that the *Horwich Chronicle* came out next week. Without doubt, their surgery would, once again, be front-page news: occupying first place in the roll call of infamous events that it had the dubious honour to have generated singlehandedly. He'd be glad that she had gone. This was the hardest thing of all. If only he'd been able to grasp, or even just accept the possibility of recognising, what was right in front of him.

The practice manager had won; Tina had lost: losing to a nasty piece of work, on the one hand, and also a woman who had died five years ago, on the other. Both had defeated her. Leaving now was her only option.

She rose to leave the room, turned as her eyes looked down at the dull floor and went back through the flimsy door. She pulled herself up to her full height, straightening her spine as she did so; knowing in that moment that this was the only way she could salvage her pride – just about the only thing left within, apart from desolation. Managing to look back just the once, seeing his head bent to the work in progress on his desk, she departed. She picked up a little cardboard box in reception and gathered her personal effects.

Several of her colleagues, those who were least cowed, looked up as she walked through reception; many had tears in their eyes. She nodded to one or two who managed to compose themselves enough to meet her gaze and then she opened the main entrance door, all without stopping. The ever-present wind howled around her as soon as she stepped outside. It tugged at her rich brown hair and jostled her slim form as if to mock her, like a bullied girl in a playground, as she departed.

As she'd closed Dr Binder's door behind her she didn't see Amanda Makepeace, practice manager, who stood at the top of the stairs just out of sight, having eavesdropped on the whole conversation. 'Little bitch was correct, all along,' she thought to herself, 'thought I'd never be able to get rid of her'. Momentary disquiet was displaced totally by a wicked, scheming smile now flooding over her face. She realised that perhaps it had been a bit of a gamble, but she knew that the senior partner could not afford to even consider the possibility that she, his practice manager, was in the wrong, let alone the vast list of things he should have been in touch with years ago. She smiled again; weak, pre-occupied men always created a vacuum; and she knew there was no space she could not seize - especially when the stakes were so high.

She strode into Dr Rapace's room. Standing very close to him, a look of undiluted satisfaction washed over her. The hem of her skirt brushed against his hand.

"Looks as though we'll be needing a new receptionist."

He smiled, the thin moustache following the movement from his thin lips causing dark eyes to pinch together.

She felt his hand stroke her leg and ascend ever higher up her thigh. She could sense his hot breath on her bare forearm as he leant forward.

"Tell me, Dr Rapace, does your wife know just what that left hand of yours gets up to?" She asked without a blink or a miss from her unperturbed heart.

"No, Mandy, and I don't plan on telling her, so perhaps keep it a secret between us two; together with all the other things we engage in when everyone's gone home?"

"Well, I suppose I couldn't possibly reveal the true activities that take place when you are working late." She became more serious as she thought aloud. "Now that Tina has gone; she is the last of the really good staff and those left behind are either stupid, or half blind to the things that have been going on."

"Well, the CCG will meet next month and hopefully we

should be ready then. Dr Binder will get his greatest wish; to go on permanent gardening leave at the age of just over forty, and give up this work that, unfortunately, he'll miss more than he knows." Fergus Rapace knew that the CCG, which had been set up as part of the latest politician-led reform of the NHS, would soon put his senior colleague out of his misery.

"When I'm in charge, Mandy, there will be a few changes around here," he offered with more oleaginous tones than even a sound stomach could sanction.

"That there will, Dr Rapace," she confirmed.

He let his hand fall as she sat on his lap, placing her hands with the long acrylic nails around his neck, squeezing him like talons as they bit into his flesh. He winced a little as she pulled him ever closer, kissing him with more force than passion, and more lust than tenderness.

Tina walked dejectedly away from the building and on through the large car park. She held the little cardboard box tightly; this being the only thing able to retain the memories that otherwise ran through her like oil through a funnel. Tears now obscured the vision in both her eyes, but she just had to look back at the place where she'd been so miserable, yet could have been so happy. The stone-built premises had been there for many years, nestling in the valley between the sheer hillsides that separated the steep fields of Bolton from those of Horwich. Weak, spring sunshine crept from its hiding place behind thick clouds, but only brought a shiver as it failed to relieve the cold that seemed to permeate from head to toe.

Her parents had told her of the days, not that long ago, when the surgery was at its height, where a new and keen young doctor had arrived, one who'd single-handedly set about making it the largest and most successful GP surgery of the West Pennine Moors. Although now, some years later, it remained busy, unhappiness and decay seemed to trickle through the entire building. It was very true, as so many had commented in hushed tones, that something of him had died that fateful day now five years ago, as had, tragically, the fortunes of the once great surgery, too.

The piercing cold wind had not quite finished with her as it whipped off the moorland, said to contain shale gas and oil that could not be recovered because of the steep slopes. Pulling the box towards her with renewed vigour, she hoped in vain that it would provide some insulation against the chill from the wind and the desolation that was reflected in those tears that she shed in a silent but unstoppable cascade. The wind of itself was biting, but when accompanied by the copious tears, her cheeks were stung like those of a polar explorer with frostbite. She passed the wooden house on her right which was at the side of the track. She saw the curtains twitch a little as she passed. No doubt Mrs Spencer, the old lady who lived there, would have noted yet another clutching a cardboard box as they, too, made the long, lonely and windy walk.

Looking up at the road, Tina saw the bus winding its way slowly round the hillside. She ran up the dirt track as fast as her weary legs would carry her so as to, hopefully, reach the stop before the bus did.

That night, Amanda Makepeace sent a confidential e-mail.

'Hi Felix, Good day today. Finally got rid of Tina Bessemer. What a clever girl she turned out to be. Thought she'd spoil the party at the last minute, so I decided to get creative. I leaked information to my contact at the local paper, who says he'll publish just how badly the surgery is doing. Then, when they mentioned their 'exclusive', I accused her of being the source of the leak. This'll be in good time for the CCG inspection next month and details our appalling rates of casualty attendances and our non-elective admissions, which are also terrible.

Everyone knows that only the two of us could have obtained this information and I knew that Binder couldn't challenge me. He thinks I'm the only way he'll get through the inspection. Little does he know the unpleasant surprise we have planned for him. Talking of little things, Fergus Rapace thinks he'll be taking over; what a rude awakening he's in for, though I may just keep him as my plaything if I don't tire of him, as I suspect I might, long before this business is over.

Which reminds me, can we meet up at weekend? I need to get my hands on a real man, not some greasy, philandering excuse for manhood. Can you tell your wife you have another out of town meeting?

I need one or two more staff. I have got rid of all those who might have guessed what's really going on here. I've been on to the medical staffing agency and they say they are scraping the barrel – little do they know it's the dregs I am looking for! They say we have interviewed all their best applicants – Lord help us, if that's the best they can do. Good job I'll be sacking them all soon enough, though I don't want to give the game away too early. Got to keep up some semblance of normality until we are ready.

Text me about our meet up? I'll book a room at our usual?
Mandy xx'

Chapter II

Hopeless Appointee

A few days later, Amanda Makepeace sat behind the desk in the meeting room silhouetted against the murky light that came in through the solitary and tiny window. She was interviewing for a new receptionist. Two of the girls had not turned up, and she flicked impatiently at the CV of the third, if the untidy document was ever to grace such a name, in front of her. She wondered if the reddish smudge in the corner was lipstick or ketchup. Once such a thought had intruded upon her she couldn't quite dismiss it from her mind. Nor, in truth, could she banish her delight at having found another eminently suitable candidate for receptionist.

She looked up distastefully at the shabby girl. A thick but well-defined eyebrow rose with incredulity above her right eye. Only shock at her appearance prevented the manager from laughing in the girl's face. The black slacks that she wore had seen better days and the shirt, though seemingly clean, was a disgusting shade, not far off mustard, which clashed violently with the auburn hair. Even this tousled mess left much to be desired: for it looked as though it had missed even fleeting contact with a comb or brush for some days, probably even longer. The long fringe hung down in a fashion that any Highland cow would have recognised. Her eyes were almost completely hidden under the haystack of hair.

Given the length of her fringe and its thickness, Mandy couldn't be sure if the girl had bothered to put on any makeup. She certainly wasn't wearing any lipstick, that was for certain,

14

unlike the manager who always chose a vivid shade of red and brought it to a high gloss finish.

She was drifting, being shocked by the girl's appearance. She couldn't hear what she was saying. In point of fact only the mumbling tones from the girl's mouth gave any clue that she was still awake. Initially Amanda tried to lean forwards in order to make an attempt to see if the girl's eyes somewhere under that fringe were in fact open, or if she'd hear snores coming from that side of the table any minute. Despite her unsettling appearance, the practice manager gave an arch smile, thinking this girl would be a perfect addition to her team. Having spotted one of life's losers at the first glimpse, Amanda decided to pay her no more heed.

She looked at the reference, which was also dreadful: 'lazy, incompetent and having a tendency to drift off even in the most pressured of environments', were words that featured heavily. She stared, once again, with incredulity at the girl's name, which had been penned in barely legible fashion: this presumably being her own handwriting. The untidy girl was perfect, and would greatly assist the practice manager with the plans that were now coming together nicely like a load of flotsam that was about to dam a river.

She coughed; it was all she could do at short notice to stifle the guffaw that would otherwise have come forth. "Well, Miss Mumple, your CV leaves a *little* to be desired, but I suppose in a surgery like ours in such a poor and run-down locality, we should not be *too* choosy. As you know, two other interviewees have not arrived, so it looks as though you are the only candidate we have. I can see, too, that your references are not the most sparkling that I've come across." Once again, she struggled to keep her face straight. An even more wicked thought then presented as she realised the dull girl probably wouldn't notice anyway. She probably wouldn't notice if that chair she was perched on suddenly gave way, she considered with even more merriment.

"You say that you have been sent by the medical staffing agency. I can see that they've had trouble placing you. All in all, I suppose beggars can't be choosers, as they say, and I expect we'll just have to give things a try and see how you get on." She coughed again so as to disable the edge of laughter.

"That's all I have to say. You can start tomorrow. Pay will be as in the enclosed sheet." Amanda looked sternly at her, thinking that under normal circumstances, she wouldn't have paid the girl in washers. However, as the malign smile rose, she knew that these times were far from normal. She'd do for now. She'd occupy space so that others would think that the manager was getting on with running the surgery, whereas in reality a very different game was in play; a strategy that was not quite ready and that needed a little confusion and camouflage for a while longer. Indeed, things were going so well that all would be revealed to all these deadbeats and losers in the not too distant future.

Miss Mumple took the sheet, and true to her name that sounded like mumble, delivered tones that were completely unintelligible to the keen-eyed practice manager.

"We'll see you here at 8:30, please, so don't be late. I'll be waiting for you. I'll see if I can give you a brief introduction to some of your colleagues and go through your duties. I note that you have worked as a receptionist before, so no doubt you won't have any trouble picking up our systems, which are very dated."

Ms Makepeace signified the end of the meeting with a dismissive wave of her hand. She didn't even glance at the new girl, her appearance causing her to be more affronted the longer she looked. Petunia Mumple mumbled more words and then left the meeting room, her steps as well as her trousers, which were far too long, shuffling over the floor. Another wicked thought entered the practice manager's mind as she wondered if their new receptionist would be able to see the door handle, let alone remember her way out of the building. Even more cruelly she entertained the image of the hapless girl getting her hem caught on the steps and disappearing down them head-first. She tittered to herself at such thoughts, but elected to remain seated while she ignored the girl, who gave new meaning to the term lacklustre, without looking up as she considered the red smudge once again. Petunia managed not only the rusty brass handle but also found, and successfully navigated, the rickety stairs which led to the ground floor.

One or two of the receptionists glanced at the new girl as she walked through reception. They, too, could recognise another hopeless appointee: one that would provide them with little by way of assistance. Without doubt, she'd be gone in such a short space of time it seemed pointless fitting her with a uniform and it would probably be a waste of breath even making an attempt to get to know her.

Petunia walked slowly back out via reception. As she did so, she saw the masses of patients queuing forlornly in the waiting room. Some had clearly been waiting for at least an hour, the length of time since she'd arrived. The distressing scene that awaited most of the patients paled beside the mood she witnessed in the reception staff. Some looked aggressively as if they were waiting to be challenged in some way; some looked frightened; and others looked completely disinterested in both their colleagues and the patients. Most had a hunted look about them, as if they worked in a climate of fear; having decided long ago that self-preservation was the only game in play. All had the air of being badly managed and of lacking even the vestiges of confidence and of pride. Much more negative attributes had clearly displaced these descriptors some time ago. Petunia wondered how long it had been since they had worked as an effective team and why the place was so busy with patients when the staff were this disinterested, some with an almost mutinous air about them. One thing impacted on her consciousness even more, however, and this was abject misery. Surely, even the most graphic of Dickensian nightmares could not be made more manifest.

Dark-panelled wooden walls seemed to complement the distressing scene. Scattered, unfiltered fluorescent tubes barely made an impact on the gloom. Along one wall were ranged tiny windows, which would never be able to begin to contribute more than a token amount of natural light even on the most sunny of summer days. Even worse, the windows had chaotic and rusty grilles tacked over them as a crime prevention measure which provided minimal deterrent against a prospective burglar but did succeed in creating even more of an oppressive air throughout. The room, though fairly large, also had a low ceiling which contributed to the unhappy ambience. The tiles that made up the suspended ceiling were tired and stained and looked as if they had not been painted since the day they were fitted. The total lack of any soft furnishings made the whole space resonate with echoes that carried sound from even the quietest of voices into the furthest reaches of the reception space.

Petunia's noiseless shuffle continued as she passed through the reception. Her flared trousers continued to scrape along the floor as she ambled forwards. She departed through the half-glazed pine doors which were coated with the same dark, dull and hastily-applied stain. As she did so, she saw tens and tens of patients filing in, each with the same expression of resigned misery – as if each of them had correctly predicted the outcome of their visit to the surgery that day.

Once she'd reached the car park, a brisk wind that whipped down from the Winter Hill transmitter found her and temporarily flicked back the unruly hair; revealing her engaging smile, clear skin and bright blue eyes that sparkled in the dull day. Keenly, she surveyed the scene, her curiosity achieving more moment on her consciousness even than the biting wind that seemed to be focussed on her. Walking a little faster, her shuffling gait changed; she picked her feet up just as she vacated the large car park. She looked behind her for as long as she dared without falling over: she stared at the impactful, rolling hills on either side which seemed to come together like the shoulders of a funnel as they met up with the car park and the extensive grounds of the premises. She continued to walk up the track that provided access to the surgery and its car park. It felt uncomfortable underfoot, the surface being covered in loose, black asphalt that had broken up into chaotic and sharp fragments. Upon her reaching the main road a little car awaited her. She opened the passenger door and jumped inside. The engine caught, as the wind picked up even more, whirring a little more insistently as the vehicle strained momentarily against its handbrake before speeding off.

The following day Petunia arrived just before 8:30 am. The practice manager waited for her in reception. Some of the patients started filing in as the doors were opened. They trudged in for the most part in complete silence. As they did so the surgery began another hesitant day: one that was now typical but nevertheless represented a pale facsimile of its former glories.

Amanda had arrived especially early and made a point of looking at her watch as the new girl wandered in. Unsettling people in this way, especially when accompanied by a piercing, distrustful look, was always a good ploy and made her staff live in fear from the outset – which was just the way she liked things. She looked skywards before looking the untidy woman up and down. Her black trousers seemed ill-fitting, almost as bad as the ones she'd had on the day before, but at least were a little shorter. Furthermore, the burgundy shirt that she'd been allocated from the surgery uniform stores suited her only marginally better than the near ochre one she had on yesterday. No doubt it would only be a matter of days before the new girl was dismissed, so there was little point in having anything altered.

"I thought I'd put you on the front desk this morning, Petunia. Do you think you'll be able to check the patients in, and also deal with their queries?" A low-volume mumble, which she could only guess was a reply of some sorts, was returned by the new receptionist to the manager, by way of an answer. "I'll return later to see how you are getting on. Any problems, then, just speak to the other girls". A spiteful smile, that she couldn't quite suppress, came over Amanda just at that moment as the thought came to her that speaking to any of these failures wouldn't get Petunia very far.

More and more people flooded in; the large waiting room was soon filled to capacity. The dark pine, wooden panelling a testament to days gone by, serving as a metaphor for the place as a whole. Dr Binder and Dr Rapace were in surgery and also two locums that had been sent by the medical staffing agency in nearby Bolton. The number of patients registered at the surgery was higher than two GPs could serve. Moreover, because Dr Binder had been unable to recruit permanent partners to work with him, the practice was dependent on short-term locums in order to provide sufficient appointments. Notwithstanding this, very soon the pressure from the people, who were queuing steadily, filled all the available slots.

Petunia looked suspiciously at the computer in front of her. She'd never seen its like before. The screen, which was barely ten inches in diameter, was an old cathode-ray-tube type of display and could only manage a shade or two of bright green as it displayed limited information on the shiny, grey-black and faded screen. The whole thing was encased in a buff-coloured, heavy plastic and this matched the keyboard, which was a massive, ungainly thing, full of dust, with fading labels applied to some of the more useful keys, and was also very weighty. Petunia picked it up as she wondered if anything so large and heavy could be just a keyboard. Pulling a little on the thick, curly lead she looked underneath it, searching for clues as to its true nature. Her right hand instinctively rested on the work top and made a reflex rotating movement but nothing was to be found there.

"Yes, I'm afraid it's pretty old kit. You won't see many computers like these. Oh, and as you've discovered there's no mouse, it's all menu driven. Must be at least twenty years old.

I'm Annabelle, by the way."

"Petunia," mumbled the new girl.

"I'll be working over here on the prescriptions, for my sins," she whispered, "but if I can help you?" she offered as she looked round to make sure that no one had overheard them. It seemed that helping each other, let alone the patients, featured nowhere in their job descriptions.

"Thank you, Annabelle, I'll shout or, perhaps, whisper if I need anything," confirmed Petunia, as she too, looked round conspiratorially, having quickly gained a sense of the usual ways of working in the surgery.

Petunia looked steadily at the indistinct, green screen, trying various key presses in an attempt to communicate with the ungainly and sluggish beast of a thing. She gave a little smile as some progress was made. Suddenly, she looked up; one or two patients were waiting quietly as they tried to guess the best way of framing their requests of the receptionists that day.

Petunia looked at the unkempt man with the check shirt standing uneasily in front of her. He was holding a little boy who, Petunia reasoned, must be about two. The child looked sweaty and lethargic. The man pointed to the little boy's ear. "It's our boy, Tim, Miss he's been unwell all night and I was hoping to get an appointment for him. He's not eating, not drinking and he seems really floppy. This liquid has been coming out of his ear all morning."

The father looked pleadingly at Petunia, but something told him that he was to be disappointed that morning, as he had been on all previous occasions when he'd attempted to get an urgent appointment. He didn't know why he'd turned up here, but the hospital was two bus rides away. The receptionist wasn't even looking at him; she was too busy looking at her keyboard and was typing furiously as she goggled at her computer screen. All he could see of her was the untidy fringe that seemed to obscure her vision completely. No doubt she used this deliberately. By such means, she would not have to see the suffering in the patients' eyes, which was palpable to all who might have occasion to take even the briefest glimpse into the room that seemed a seething hotbed of unfulfilled requests and disappointment. Suddenly, the girl looked up; eyes shone from beneath the fringe as Petunia gazed at the worried father unfalteringly.

"Yes, of course. I'm sorry to hear about his poorly ear, and he doesn't look at all well. May I have Tim's second name and date of birth?" The father paused for a moment. He dared to believe that his request was about to be actioned.

"Green, Miss, born 6th June 2015."

"Thank you. Mr Green, if you could just take a seat please. Dr Binder's surgery is full, but if you can give me just a minute, I will ask him if he'll be able to see Tim."

The father's mouth fell open, but no words came forth. He'd been stunned by the kindness, and especially the concern, expressed for his little boy by the receptionist that had temporarily disconnected his speech. He did manage a nod, however, as his mouth remained open. He did as he was asked. He was further rewarded by a dazzling smile from the receptionist just before it was eclipsed by the dense fringe that intervened quickly.

Petunia picked up the phone. Susan, one of her colleagues who had been working in the computer next to her, touched her hand quickly.

"I wouldn't do that if I were you. Instructions from Ms Makepeace are that once the surgeries are full, then the doctors are not to be disturbed. She'll go ape if she finds out that you've agreed to a request that an *extra* is seen. Usually, we just tell them to go to casualty."

"But surely, Susan," Petunia looked quickly at the receptionist's name badge as she spoke, "that's five miles away and that little boy looks really ill, don't you think?"

"Look, Petunia, is it? You are new here; if you want to survive, then you'd better wise up. It's *not* our concern. The *patients* are not our concern. *She* will have your guts for garters if you cross her." Her eyes mirrored the cowed and frightened expression that was set on her face. For a moment panic intervened as she saw Petunia avert her gaze for a second and she wondered if the manager was behind her. "She's got rid of far better people than you, trust me. In fact, she gets rid of *anyone* who goes up against her; and the key to keeping your job here is to nod and do *exactly* what she tells you. You'll be for it if you upset her." Susan now nodded as if to emphasise her point to the new girl.

"Well, Susan, I'm just going to have to take that risk." She displayed a more confident smile than she could manage inwardly. Mercifully, her colleague could not see that her legs were shaking.

Petunia put the phone down and moved down the dark corridor that smelt of dry rot, presumably from the wooden panelling that had seen better days. She waited until his patient came out and then knocked on Dr Binder's door.

"Forgive me, Dr Binder. I have a Master Green out in the waiting room; he does not look at all well and his father is asking for an urgent appointment?"

Dr Binder looked up quickly from typing up his notes for the previous patient.

"Yes, yes of course, give me two minutes and then send them straight in. I know the little boy, his dad has not long since lost his job and his wife has just walked out on them both."

"Thank you so much, Dr Binder, I will inform the father and will show them down, if I may, in a couple of minutes?"

"And so, tell me, my dear, just who are you?" The kind, almost paternal, smile appeared all too briefly but was, nonetheless, directed at the young woman. Shiny brown eyes, like polished snooker balls, looked enquiringly at the receptionist before they too seemed to be dulled by the veneer of sadness.

"I'm Petunia Mumple, Dr Binder, I've just started."

"Thank you for approaching me with this, Petunia." His smile re-appeared for a moment as he engaged with her breezy manner and those brilliant blue eyes that seemed imprisoned by an unruly fringe. She smiled before pausing just for a moment as she rapidly made a mental note and confirmed something that she'd suspected all along. The brief grin was lost; the sadness came back to claim him and Petunia went to find the patient and his father in order to show them in to Dr Binder's consulting room.

Twenty minutes later, the GP appeared at the front desk.

"I just wanted to thank you, Petunia, for being so sharp. Poor Tim has mastoiditis and I need to send him to hospital. I phoned the Paediatric ENT on-call and they will see him now. Many thanks, Petunia, it would have been very nasty if there had been a delay."

The fringe nodded, but the smile and the bright eyes lay hidden. She did manage, however, a low pitch mumble to the effect that it was her pleasure.

As soon as the GP had gone, Susan approached her once again.

"You be very careful. If *she* gets to hear of this, she'll be down on you like a ton of bricks, and don't think *he* will save you. He's in so much trouble with the CCG, it's well known if she walks they will close him down. You seem like a nice person and I admire what you did," once again fear crossed over the receptionist like a ghost covering a grave. "It's just that if you value your job here, mark my words." She made a sign with her finger like a knife crossing her throat.

"Well, let's hope she doesn't find out, then." Petunia replied, managing only a fleeting moment of confidence that couldn't be sustained.

Susan shook her head, frustrated at the price paid by those naïve enough to think that they could do the right thing in this surgery. For with jobs being scarce in the town Petunia would learn, possibly the hard way, that it was all about survival and had nothing to do with offering a service to the patients. Susan thought to herself that it was a shame, as the new girl seemed friendly and hard-working. She also had a nice, caring attitude, surely what the job under normal conditions needed. Trouble was things were not normal; they were far from being so. Petunia would find out too late, for sure, that the manager would tolerate none of those attributes and she would be dismissed long, long before she would be able to make any friends. Viewed in this light, Susan reasoned that there would be little point in talking to her, as she would probably not be employed more than a few days. A grisly image came to her; it was a little bit like a getting to know a prisoner on death row.

That afternoon, Matilda Spencer arrived in good time for her appointment. Petunia checked her details on the green-screen computer. The cursor flashed insistently at the place where patient details were held, but, apart from this, abandoned any pretence at either speed or efficiency. The receptionist had mastered the use of the long line of function keys, which would have to be memorised then invoked in order to summon even one of the hundreds of menus that would have to be navigated in order to obtain any co-operation at all from the out-dated system.

Petunia recognised her address, having noted the little cottage, for it was at the very end of the long lane that went up from the surgery, just round the corner from where it joined the main road; where the bus stop was situated. The young woman had also guessed where her passions lay by the assorted cat ornaments and paraphernalia, which adorned the outside walls of the building. More evidence became available, when she caught the slight feline whiff as she stood talking to the elderly lady across the worn Formica desktop.

"Hello, Mrs Spencer, what a lovely Christian name you have," remarked the receptionist as she showed her dazzling smile, which had hitherto lain hidden under the untidy fringe. "I have checked you in," she confirmed, while nimble fingers clacked over the clumsy, un-cooperative and ancient keyboard. "I don't think you'll be waiting long, though Dr Binder is running a little late."

"And who might you be, my dear?" asked the keen-eyed older lady.

"I'm Petunia, Mrs Spencer, new receptionist."

"Well, I do hope you'll stay a bit longer than most of the girls do," Mrs Spencer commented, bending forwards as much as she was able in order to take in more of the pretty face and dazzling smile that was on offer below the disordered fringe; to all those who took the time to look for it.

"Poor Dr Binder, he's not been very lucky. Things have gone from bad to worse since that terrible day." The patient nodded knowingly at the young woman who seemed puzzled. Embarrassment precluded further speech. She sensed that she was about to burden the girl with more information than was wise, especially as her blank look indicated she was in ignorance of the horrors that the GP had weathered. Electing to change the subject quickly, she continued. "He is such a caring, marvellous doctor. I know, when I come here, that he will sort me out. I've a terrible noise in my ears, you see."

Petunia nodded as she had heard of tinnitus, which she understood to be ringing in one's ears.

"Funny though, it only comes on at night and it makes this noise like an engine, but in my head. It's there only when I am in bed at night and it's gone by morning." The receptionist smiled again but sensed that she was now out of her depth, and was grateful when Dr Binder called Matilda's name over the Tannoy.

"Nice to meet you, Mrs Spencer, and good luck with your noise."

"Oh, he'll soon have me sorted, he is a wonderful doctor, and what a kind man. That's the only reason why this place is still here."

Matilda hesitated for a minute as she looked again at the girl's enthusiastic glimmer, bright smile and pleasant demeanour.

"Good luck in your new job, Petunia, and I do hope we meet again," the elderly lady offered with a whimsical smile.

"That's so kind of you, Mrs Spencer, I hope so too."

Matilda nodded, as relief overcame her that she hadn't said too much to the young woman. Without doubt, the youth of today were incapable of compassing tragedy, especially of the depth that had engulfed the senior GP. "Look after yourself now, Petunia, won't you?"

"I'll do my best, Mrs Spencer, nice to meet you today." The young woman's voice went up a little as she compensated for the noise in reception and the distance that opened as the patient moved towards the consulting room.

"Likewise, my love."

She walked towards the consulting room with a bemused but knowing look. Thinking to herself what a wonderful young woman she'd met. She was then compelled to wonder, in turn, just how long she'd last in a surgery that seemed to lose its workforce like troops making a hasty charge on a cannon battery.

As Mrs Spencer moved away from reception Petunia's long fingers, once again, danced over the lifeless keyboard. Her fingers could move so much more quickly than either the keyboard or computer could respond. She arrived at the reporting menu, only after a succession of counter-intuitive key presses on the sticky keys: her right hand, in particular, missing the mouse, which the computer would not be able to address even if one had been supplied. The reporting menu flared in front of her, just a little hazy, but nonetheless present, on the ghostly green screen. She could see the array of reports that were available: some pre-defined, others unique to the surgery, now listed and extending well beyond the bottom of the visible screen. She became aware of one of the other receptionists moving behind her and quickly pressed the 'Escape' key in order to banish the list and return the monitor to its favoured dormant state, the fading grey-black hue now returning as the green text vanished.

Pressure from the patients continued for the remainder of the afternoon; eventually closing time was upon them and the girls began to drift home. Petunia found herself sitting alone in the office. The cleaners arrived and soon dispersed throughout the building, as they got on with their familiar routine. The practice manager appeared unexpectedly in the office, clearly surprised to see her.

"What are you still doing here, Miss Mumple?" she queried in a suspicious and far from friendly tone.

Petunia offered indistinctly that she was in the process of closing her machine down and mumbled further that she wished the manager a 'good evening' as she collected her coat.

Amanda Makepeace entered Dr Rapace's room and closed it firmly behind her. Despite this, Petunia heard muffled sounds, which left little doubt in her mind as to the reason for such a late meeting, as she hurriedly left via the front door.

Dr Rapace remained seated as Amanda approached him, an odd, ravenous look in her eye.

"Oh, I see you are working late again, Doctor." She stood next to him, her legs stretching back against the pencil skirt so as to cause the mid-thigh split to reveal more than a hint of the lacy tops of her hold-up stockings.

"Yes I am, Ms Makepeace, at least that's what I have told my wife." At this he inserted his palm between her legs and slowly swept it upwards.

"Let's see then, what have we here?" she said, as she moved even further towards him, brushing his hand away violently, and then began to remove his clothing with more force than finesse, and more desperation than desire.

Chapter III

Punishment Room

The following day Petunia was placed in the filing room. Amanda Makepeace was waiting for her, once again, as she arrived. The manager was, almost, able to defeat the spiteful and punitive grin that had assembled on her expression. It was time for the new girl to learn who was in charge at her new place of work. The manager had learned long ago that breaking people had to begin almost immediately, rather like crushing rubble to create a nice smooth pathway. She knew that this was the ideal time for a demonstration of what could befall those who were now subject to the whims of a superior who was determined that none of them should forget their place – under her boot: preferably shaking with fear at all times.

Amanda had prepared such a place, rather like sailors in wooden ships of old who had been confined to the horrors of the Orlop deck, where screaming, half-crazed men would have yard-long wooden splinters, as well as shattered limbs, removed – without anaesthetic. The manager had determined that it was time for the new girl to feel its full effect. From this point on the new receptionist would know exactly where she stood: at the very bottom. What was more, just about anything unpleasant could and would be visited upon her, and any of the others, at a moment's notice.

The other girls remained hushed, not daring to make eye-contact as Petunia was led away, like a prisoner to a stretch of solitary confinement. Petunia shuffled along docilely following the practice manager like a sheep dog in need of a good shearing as her fringe bounced along in front of her.

Most GP surgeries, up and down the land, had been encouraged to move exclusively to computerised scanning and filing of patient letters, electronic transfers and patient records. However, the West Pennine surgery retained manual systems. The ancient and inadequate computer system was barely able to keep up with appointments, prescriptions and limited clinical notes, let alone anything remotely resembling modern practices that had swept through the NHS. Almost as a monument to times now gone, the crude system backed by these antediluvian methods had failed to keep up with the sheer volume of correspondence from a variety of sources. The consequence of this was a vast volume of post and paper that had never even come close to the patients' notes where it belonged.

The filing room bore untidy and frightening testament to such practices. It was a large room, but this only served to enhance its cluttered and oppressive atmosphere with little natural light and lots of dust from paper and files that continued to amass daily. The low ceiling, covered in cracked and yellowing ceiling panels, was a perfect accompaniment to the miserable space.

Post would be delivered daily to the surgery; a large, inked stamp would then be applied to each page. The doctors would then read it and tick or initial the relevant box in the imprint so formed either for further action, or, at its most simple, for it to be passed to the filing room.

Only when all these steps had been completed was the letter ready for filing. Unfortunately, this was only the beginning. Several more steps then followed, in that each of the patient case-note files would have to be pulled from the filing shelves, the piece of paper punched and eventually filed. The notes would then be repositioned on the shelves by matching pairs of numbered tracer cards to ensure that they were retained in the correct order.

The chaotic, oppressive and dingy atmosphere in the room gave a clue as to the nature of the work: it being amongst the least favourite of the long list of such things that all of the girls quietly abhorred within. Investigations such as X-ray reports and blood tests would also have to be filed and, because of their small size, could only be positioned within the notes by the use of special mount sheets which would keep similar groups of successive results together. Most vitally, the filing was so far behind schedule that it was rarely possible to find a letter when it was required because it was more often than not buried, somewhere, in the deepening chaos. More days than not a receptionist would be despatched to the filing room in order to find a crucial letter and the whole place would often be turned over while she looked for the sought-after letter. This in turn created a vicious cycle and a gathering momentum for disarray with the ever-present danger of something really vital going astray.

More than this, if a doctor needed an urgent letter or laboratory report, then both he and the patient would have to wait for the receptionist to enter and search the filing room. This in turn diverted receptionists from the front desk and held up the surgeries as well as adding to the chaos within the miserable room.

Petunia entered with something approaching fear, as a man who couldn't swim perhaps would experience on entering water that he thought was of paddle depth, only to discover that he had been immersed well over his head. Wire racks and trays were strewn everywhere. Each was filled to bursting with correspondence that a succession of receptionists, who were terrified of losing their jobs, had judged would surely be done one day but, unfortunately, not today. Temporary and disinterested staff had many other pressures placed on their shoulders and had more urgent aims, like keeping their jobs, to consider. The words 'chaos reigned' had never seemed so apposite.

Amanda held the door open for the receptionist like an executioner leading the way to the gallows, but then left with a light-hearted spring in her step as another victim was about to be shown what misery could be inflicted on the manager's underlings arbitrarily and by an unfeeling whim. At first, as panic established itself, Petunia gasped for breath. This in turn engendered feelings that she was choking and the dry, dusty and chaotic atmosphere within the filing room was perfect for exaggerating such thoughts.

Petunia's momentary panic settled, however, as her agile mind quickly formulated a strategy. Mercifully, there remained several feet of clear worktop space and she seized on this as being central to her plan. She set to work. All the trays were upended and turned out on to the work surface. Using the space available, she soon created piles of paper sorted into alphabetical groups. She found a couple of ageing, rubber thimbles which she applied to a finger of each hand. This sped up her paper handling significantly and also, at least partially, protected her fingers as she sped through the sheets.

More full trays were then selected and their contents added in turn to the piles of paper now rising steadily on the work-surface. Once they had been separated in this way, each group was then brought into alphabetical order, long, responsive fingers being deployed to rapidly bring this about. Once this initial step was accomplished, it was then an easier matter to file the letters in the notes. As each letter was now in order, as one was filed the one below it would be for a set of notes to be located adjacent, or at least nearby, on the shelves. The results and x-rays were separated from the main correspondence and this process would then be repeated, these having to be glued onto the mount sheets.

After a couple of hours, deceptively fast movements and intense concentration had brought some clear space as well as a little daylight into the room; at last some progress was being made. Having cleared a little space, and as more daylight entered, Petunia discovered that the window could be opened, thereby allowing a little fresh air to dilute the dusty miasma.

Some time later the practice manager appeared suddenly and noiselessly, which was a trick that needed significant care, as she nearly always sported very high shoes on sizeable feet. Petunia gave a little jump, the long, untidy fringe dancing in front of her as she did so.

"Just what are you doing?" demanded the manager.

"I thought you wanted me to do some filing?"

"But *how* have you managed to clear so much so quickly?" she asked accusingly, sensing that she must have had help in order to liberate so much space in such a short interval of time.

Petunia didn't need to look too closely to gain a sense that the manager was surprised, suspicious and annoyed in increasing significance and mounting intensity. Amanda's thoughts had quickly moved on to discovering the culprit who must have given assistance so that she could be summarily fired for her trouble. Surely no one person could have done so much so quickly. She looked round the room warily.

"Oh, I don't think there was as much as we thought," Petunia replied with neither hesitation nor a mumble, for once.

Dark eyes continued to bore into the young receptionist with mounting aggression. It seemed from the close scrutiny that was put upon her that the receptionist was telling the truth. This unsettled the manager more. She'd been hoping to berate her for hardly making an impact on what lay within, the poison chalice that she'd been given, and here in complete contrast she had discovered a task that was well on its way to completion. The manager had to get away to assess this unforeseen set of circumstances, certainly not what she'd expected from the no-hoper that she'd taken on.

"Well, it's time for your break, perhaps do some more later," were the alternative words to the ones she'd planned and, with that, she turned and was gone. Later, back in reception, the practice manager glared at the young woman for some time. Suspicion and alarm rose within, fed by the wide disparity between the new girl's speech, her appearance and the speed with which she could accomplish tasks that were mostly beyond the other receptionists. She made a mental note that all was not what it appeared and, without doubt, neither was this new girl. She knew, too, that her instincts were rarely wrong in such matters. Ms Makepeace had spent a lifetime in using these instincts to disadvantage and crush all those who found themselves near her. A much worse fate awaited those who dared to cross her than those who failed because of their own inadequacies.

A short time later, Amanda was seen leaving the reception area and entering Dr Rapace's room after adjusting her slim pencil-skirt and black patent belt with a large, rectangular chromed buckle.

The following day, Petunia was placed on reception to greet patients and make sure their arrival was entered laboriously on the inflexible computer system. Although dealing with a steady stream of anxious patients, she couldn't fail to spot a long and restless queue that had formed at the side of the front desk. This was where repeat prescription requests were made and collected.

Annabelle, who was manning this station, had an unsettled look, verging on panic. She continued to touch her own forehead and rubbed at her eyes as a wave of distress washed over her with mounting force. Her pale features had long since taken on a bright-pink hue as she fought with the stress and embarrassment. The patients queued steadily: some coughed, some stared and some shifted their feet aimlessly. One or two looked more hostile. All looked deeply unhappy as if their instinct and previous experience had already prepared them for a significant and fruitless wait.

"Sorry, your repeat prescription isn't ready yet." Annabelle offered the, by now, habitually repeated words.

"But, Miss, I ordered it last week, and I ran out of tablets yesterday," the patient beseeched, with a feeling that his breath had just been wasted.

"I'm sorry but you'll have to come back, perhaps tomorrow?" she suggested, hoping, vainly, that the simple and inadequate words would somehow have more conviction than she could feel inside. The disappointed and frustrated patient moved away as another replaced him. The unhappy line inched forward and a similar request followed.

"*My* little boy ran out of his inhalers, and I *also* made my request last week. I was told I could collect them today?"

The hapless receptionist then looked forlornly through the little tray for a completed request. But she knew, before she began, that she would not find it. Those who queued in front of her knew it too. Breaking eye-contact, she gave a little hysterical laugh, shrugged her shoulders and prepared to disappoint yet another patient. Before words could form, however, Petunia tapped her carefully on the shoulder. Annabelle turned round to see the new girl standing next to her. She shook her head, any panic now having dissipated into a strange mix of defiance, apathy and surrender.

"We just haven't had the time to do them," she said, as much to herself as to her colleague and the people who looked intensely at her.

"Can I help you?" asked Petunia, brightly.

Annabelle stared at the new girl. It was a long time since she'd heard those words. Those who had the temerity to use them had, to a woman, been dismissed: for it had long-since taken on the dimensions of a beef farmer appearing at a vegetarian conference. Her first instinct was to laugh and ask her just what she thought she could do; so disempowered and cowed had all the staff become. Then she looked round to see if anyone else had noticed the dangerous words that had just been uttered.

Annabelle looked again, more carefully this time, at her colleague; seeing the dazzling blue eyes glow under the fringe, like sunshine dispelling a cold autumnal day; the full lips parted to reveal a bright smile that offered not only friendship and support but also a competence. More than this,

Petunia's demeanour held the promise of so much more than her physical presence, as the new girl stood next to her. Annabelle couldn't help but smile back; something that was widely and routinely crushed in the girls' working day. She dared. For the first time in many months, she dared; and so it was: hope formed. Patients, too, stared, now almost holding their breath as Petunia beamed back, a little hesitantly at first, but with growing confidence.

"May I?" she began, as Annabelle moved to one side. Petunia addressed the keyboard. Resistant keys went 'clackety-clack' as they were pressed to a speed of response that few had summoned from them ever before. The prescription menu came up and glowed docilely, like a badly-behaved dog sensing the arrival of its rightful master. Then the voice came forth with clarity and a deeper register than Annabelle had hitherto heard from her colleague.

Turning to Annabelle, she asked. "If you could take the names of the first twenty in the queue and either take from them their request slip or find it in the box, and please place them here in the order of their position in the queue, I'll do the rest." Blue eyes fired, like the apex of the flame from a Butane blowtorch at its hottest point, as they temporarily emerged from the fringe that habitually eclipsed them.

Petunia pulled herself up to her full height, having subconsciously prepared herself for the task in hand. Each patient was addressed by name as they strode forwards. All were rewarded with steadfast eye contact and utmost professionalism. Petunia's eyes were now glowing with delight, but remained largely obscured by the fringe as the patients approached in turn.

First, each received an apology; then they were informed that their prescription would be available to them in approximately five minutes if they would just care to take a seat.

As each moved forward, menu-driven systems were set in motion at a speed never before seen as each prescription was generated as quickly as the computer was capable of responding. Old printers, that had seen better days, were then placed under a deluge of print requests as prescription after prescription issued forth.

As soon as the first twenty were ready for signing, Petunia scooped them from the printer tray and was already folding them and placing them in order, ready for signing. She then took the small bundle, so created, and moved to Dr Binder's consulting room.

Annabelle stared after her with a mixture of incredulity and horror. She knew that such things were not only unheard of in the miserable surgery but also that anyone daring to espouse such a helpful manner would be through the door with a small box containing her effects as soon as it came within the sphere of knowledge of their manager.

Still in blissful ignorance of such things, as she went down the pine-panelled corridor, Petunia continued to group and fold them. By so doing she hoped that their checking and signing would be as uncomplicated as possible. She readied herself to wait outside the muddy-brown, dull door but mercifully the patient had just departed and it had been left ajar. She knocked against the open portal and went straight in, holding the little bundle in front of her.

"Forgive me, Dr Binder, but we have a bit of a backlog in reception and I wonder if you'd be able to sign these for me? I am sorry to inconvenience you in this way. I have checked them all and they are all either due or, in some case, overdue."

His head was raised and sad eyes looked at her; as they did so they glanced on their travel to fall on the little frame on his desk, which redoubled his sadness. He rubbed the ring on his left hand a little nervously while the bright young woman waited, shimmering with enthusiasm, before him. From somewhere, deep within his ennui, a flicker of a smile formed, for there was something compelling about her breezy manner and facilitatory demeanour.

"Ah, Miss Mumple isn't it? So, what can I do for you?" the kindness in his voice not quite being translated despite the best efforts of his expression.

She showed him the small wad of prescriptions, apologised again for troubling him and confessed as to the disarray on the prescription counter.

"Ah, I see, yes, yes of course, please let me have them."

He whisked through the signatures in rapid succession. She collected them from him and turned to go with a further flash of her bright smile, like a beam from a lighthouse keeping ships clear of the rocks.

"Doctor, would you be offended if I wait outside in a few minutes so that you can sign some more? I am afraid there is a bit of a queue and I am hoping to get it cleared."

He nodded, but his thoughts paused with a dilemma. Why was it that nobody ever asked him for assistance in this way if queues were forming in reception? His mind could supply no answers, but without further delay he smiled, just a little, as he nodded once more. By this time a more pressing query had come to him.

"Petunia, who are you?" he asked, a quizzical look overtaking, even then, the sadness etched to his face.

"Just as I said, I'm the new girl, Dr Binder. A young woman hoping to earn an honest crust, nothing more." He nodded with recognition of her words, but he knew that something had neither been asked nor said. In the days ahead he would clarify some of that missing information.

Petunia walked briskly from his room in order to find all the patients who had been asked to take a seat. They looked at the prescription as they held it like a golden ticket that they'd just found in a chocolate bar. Most smiled, some remained numb as well as dumb, a few expressed their gratitude summoning words as they did so, but all were grateful to this young woman who'd clearly gone out of her way for them. Some would mutter as they walked from the surgery clutching the precious green forms she'd handed to them that it was like the old days – almost. Days when the surgery had been a friendly, happy place that served its patients, all of them, at all times, come rain or shine. How they missed those days and the man whose energy and enthusiasm had promulgated those times.

Petunia then repeated the whole process until the queue had emptied. By this time a small queue of patients waiting to be checked in had formed at the front desk and she made ready to return so that neither patient nor doctor was kept waiting. Before she did so, however, she noted the plastic box which still contained hundreds of prescription requests. She suggested to her colleague that they try to action some of the requests in the box so that they would not have to go through the same fire-fighting approach they had all just endured. This would mean, in turn, that in future they would be ahead of events.

In that moment, as soon as the entirely reasonable suggestion left her lips, she saw real fear totally subsume her colleague's expression.

"Ms Makepeace says we should only do them once a patient comes in, and that we have far too much on to mollycoddle them all in this way; that they will only come to expect it. She tells us that Dr Binder has given specific instructions to this effect – did he not shout at you when you went in there?"

Petunia smiled politely, she now understood just a little more. She touched the girl's arm gently by way of acknowledging the pressures they were all under. No further words were said as she returned to her station.

It was to be just before mid-day, when the surgery had calmed a little, that Susan tapped Petunia on the shoulder.

"You are playing a very dangerous game. I realise you are trying to help the patients," the unaccustomed word stuck a little in her throat as she voiced it, "but, if she finds out she will sack you in a heartbeat. I don't know why but she wants this place on its knees crawling along. Anyone, anyone who tries to get it off its knees is fired, just like that," Susan turned round to make sure the manager had not crept into the office and, seeing the coast was clear, clicked her fingers. "Just like that, and they are history. We all need these jobs and, forgive me, but by looking at you," she looked Petunia up and down, "I figure that you need this job, too. I think it's good what you are trying to do but many have tried before and all, all have departed. Got rid of by her." she raised a thumb and used it to indicate a space that existed just over her shoulder: a space that represented a killing field of misery to all who might come to the attention of the manager within. She looked round again as if just thinking about this particular devil would make her manifest.

"Susan, thank you for warning me. I just have to do what I have to do. They deserve so much better," she nodded towards the waiting room in which sat one or two patients, "and so do you. All of you." Petunia had raised her voice, so much so that many turned and looked at the usually quiet and indistinct new girl.

"It's no good, Petunia, don't say I didn't warn you. When she drops on you, you won't know what's hit you. I have seen it again and again." Susan shook her head dejectedly as she grappled, not for the first time, with how things were and the realisation that little would change.

"Thank you, Susan, I know you mean well."

Susan moved away, fearing that more words of caution might well see both of them being sacked. She had delivered her warning to the new girl and she could only wonder what could be a higher priority than self-preservation. She shrugged her shoulders.

Dr Rapace had finished his surgery and Amanda Makepeace had entered his room. She leant against the desk, her eyes aflame, as if she was about to devour the GP as he sat facing her. Far from relishing the attention he sat, rubbing his neck, his back and his thighs; his face contorted with pain as he did so.

"You were so rough last night," he began.

"I thought that was the way you liked it? Does Mrs Rapace not provide you with all the things that I can, then?" Although she pitched her words as a question the emphasis as she stood there staring at him hungrily was laden with more rhetoric than otherwise.

"Not quite," he confessed, as he continued to find new painful areas to rub.

Her gaze was suddenly averted as she changed the subject. "I don't like that new girl. She's up to no good." As she voiced the words her nails with the acrylic extensions bit into the soft flesh of his neck just a little more, causing him to flush and perspire. He could feel her hot breath on his neck as she then came closer.

"What do you mean?" he offered, as he looked at the CV she'd given him.

Amanda occupied the patient chair as he looked through the file, the slit in her skirt parting to reveal muscular thighs and the glistening tops of her black hold-ups.

"She's just a bit too keen – efficient, even. She wants to help the patients and also to get things done: all the things that will get this surgery a good name, if we aren't careful," she said with neither irony nor shame. "Just when we are almost ready. I haven't spent all this time bringing this place ... sorry, *we* haven't spent all this time destroying this place from the inside out for some stupid girl to frustrate us. She even managed to cope with the filing room," she said, with disgust forming on the cherry-red lipstick that glistened, somehow, in the subdued lighting of his consulting room.

He smiled as he handed back the file. "Ah yes, your punishment room. I don't think anyone with a CV like that will be able to frustrate our plans at this, the eleventh hour, when we are almost done. We must be close enough, now, so as to be unstoppable - especially by some *slip* of a girl."

"No, perhaps you are right, but she gives me an uneasy feeling."

"I thought nothing gave you uneasy feelings."

"More true than you realise, lover, but I'll be watching her just the same, and she can always go the same way as the rest of those who thought they could outsmart me."

"I can't see that happening this side of the second coming."

"Too right. Anyway, what I came to tell you is that the bank has been in touch with me. They say that your offer of £100,000 for the old cinema in Horwich village centre has been accepted. You'll need to guarantee at least this amount and a further 100k for the building work needed and, not forgetting, the conversion. This said, however, builders are ready to begin almost immediately."

He nodded, but was plunged into thoughts of his own. "Well, I'll have to put my house up as surety, at least until the cost rent application has been made and I can then access Government grants designed to assist GPs who create new surgeries. As soon as we are up and running this place can be closed down."

This reminded him of something he'd been meaning to ask. His brow furrowed and the thin but dark eyebrows knotted together like a pair of seagull's wings.

"Why is it we couldn't just stay here when we've got rid of old misery guts?"

Somewhere, along the tortuous line of deception, he'd obviously missed something.

Her eyes changed from a look of passion to one of pure avarice. She uncrossed her legs revealing now even more of her stocking tops and acres of glossy and toned thigh.

"Look, he *owns* this building – he could simply hang on if he wanted to, especially if he wanted to be bloody-minded. Now, once he's failed his inspection and the CCG have rendered him *non-viable*, they'll all flock to register with you. Only once he sees it's all over will he give up the ghost – whoops, so to speak. Oh well, no, I don't think he'll ever give up the ghost," she laughed viciously, "but you know what I mean. You can then buy this place for peanuts."

"What would I want it for? I'll have enough loans round my neck."

"Okay then, I thought you'd say that, I might just put him out of his misery and buy it off him," she said, doing her best to make it appear as an afterthought.

"*You*, on *your salary* with what we pay you!"

"Oh, don't you worry it'll go for a song and I reckon I'll be ready for a pay rise."

"We'll see. I suppose that depends on just what services you offer me."

She gripped him by his throat, her eyes darkening with menace. "I would have thought I've offered you more *service* than one man can possibly handle. I can't think you've been in any way short-changed. Or am I mistaken?" She'd moved with the speed of a cobra striking, in reaching for his neck, but the bite was that of the nails as sharp as fangs. As she tightened her grip they bit into the flesh of his throat just enough to break the skin. He had been more than startled by the speed of her approach but his reflexes had been incapable of pulling back in time. He struggled but realised this would only cause more pain and bleeding from the cuts in his neck. Dark eyes flared as she came nearer and her grip only relaxed when she saw fear appear in his eyes: just the way she liked it.

He coughed a little, before attempting speech, grateful for his escape from more pain. He rubbed his neck in an attempt both to sooth it and also to disperse the blood before it stained his collar.

"Well, you seem to know what you are doing," he said as he continued to rub his throat, so much so that it muffled some of his words.

"Oh yes, you'd better believe it," she replied with a tone in her voice that was laced even more with aggression than her typical state of overbearing confidence. "Then you can sack this lot of losers." She laughed as she thought of the fools that lay around her. Only at this point did the fury in her eyes subside a little. She looked, now, over his shoulder as she stared into her vision of the future.

"A few interviews for some *decent* staff, bring in doctors you *really* want to work with," she suggested.

"Or, better" he cut in, "I think I'd bring in salaried doctors and a few nurse practitioners, work them all like stink and rake off all the profits while I pay my exorbitant loans down. If you are really good I may just keep you on as the provider of extra services for me."

She touched the top of her chest with her flattened palm and rocked back ostentatiously on her heels as she stood.

"Well, aren't I the lucky one! Just what did I do to deserve all of this," her hands moved around the room expansively as she mocked him.

"Don't worry, when I am running the show I won't forget who my friends are."

"So, that's just me, then," she offered with more truth than he felt comfortable with. He became quiet as if the undiluted truth had triggered something of a re-appraisal.

She sensed his angst, but knew she had to keep him on side and compliant, at least for now. Her eyes glowed again as one of her legs came forward through the slit in her skirt in order to rub against his leg. She coaxed it back and forth against his suit trousers, "Next time you are working late I might just do that special thing you like."

He pulled her to him, gripping her hips with his hands now sweating just a little as the passion rose.

That night Amanda made her excuses and left work earlier than usual. Upon arriving home, she sent a further email from her computer.

'Hi Felix,

It's all in place! The sale of the new premises has gone through. The builders should begin this week. I should be able to make my move as soon as he fails his inspection. Given the nasty things that will come to light as soon as they take even a quick look, it won't take long.

I have to work late tonight so as to make at least a token effort and give them something to look through when they come. As soon as our bid goes in, in order to continue to provide general medical services they'll definitely render Binder non-viable. The 'bid' I am putting together won't stay afloat any longer than a rusty bath tub with a few holes in. Likewise, it should sink without trace. Fool won't know what's hit him. Talking of fools, that sick bastard Rapace says he *might* just keep me on. I can't wait to see his face when he finds out who is really in charge round here – and he's really been working for me, all along. I can't wait for weekend so we can meet up? Need a real man, and a real lover not some weak excuse for such.

Shall we meet at our usual rendezvous again? I'd better go and get on with my reports. The sooner I can get them under the noses of some pretty powerful people, the sooner I can be free of the, ever so tearful, Dr Binder and the really creepy, two timing, 'gift to womanhood', Rapace.'

Chapter IV

After Hours Meeting

The following day Petunia had been banished, once more, to the filing room. She'd spent all day within its claustrophobic confines, but at last every scrap of paper had been identified, sorted and inserted in its correct place. The filing had not been up to date for at least five years. She looked round the room, just before she switched the light off, with some pride and satisfaction. If they could only keep on top of it then the staff should have no more problems with missing letters and reports. She closed the door and went into the office, noting that everyone had gone home. Only one or two cleaners busied themselves about the building as they got on with the vacuuming and cleaning as best they could. They muttered as they went about their difficult work that the dark, dilapidated premises had seen better days and less and less of the effort they put in was making any difference at all.

Petunia remained in the office and began tidying one or two prescriptions, delighted to discover that Annabelle had made a valiant effort in reducing the pile of the ones that were yet to be processed. With a little encouragement, who knew what they might accomplish.

After a short time she looked at her watch and moved to the side door to unbolt it. A few minutes later there came a quiet tap. As she opened the door with care a tall figure was revealed standing there in the early evening, clutching a laptop and a packet of blank A4 paper. He hesitated briefly on the threshold; the wind whipped off the moorland doing its best to push against the door as it was carefully and quietly closed. This accomplished, she fell into his arms, having to stand on her tip-toes in order to kiss him as he entered.

"Hello my darling, are you okay?" he asked.

"Always, always. I'm fine, now that you are here, thanks for asking, but it's been a long few days. I've never seen a place like it."

He looked round the dismal room, his eyes focussing, in particular, on the antiquated computers.

"My goodness, haven't seen computers like these since I was ten, I think," he concluded, a worried look appearing on his face as he considered whether they would be able to get the information they needed.

"Whoosh, it's like going back twenty years, I can tell you. I can see I have my work cut out here."

She nodded in full agreement. Even the smile that readily appeared on her bright face when she looked at him was temporarily banished. "You should try using them when the place is busy. That's real fun! It's as we were told. Certainly it's as bad as we feared – maybe even worse. The poor soul, Dr Binder, is surrounded by the demoralised, those who can't wait to stab him in the back, and one who singlehandedly redefines the meaning of cruelty."

"That pleasant, eh?" he concluded as he nodded sympathetically, temporarily stalled by the oppressive atmosphere that seemed to permeate throughout the entire premises. He shivered from head to toe and thought that only some of this was due to the cold wind that came off the moors as he'd waited.

"Okay, let's make a start shall we? Time is pressing and we need to have an idea of what we're really up against."

"I managed to get in to the reporting menu. It's a little crude, but it will do, and contains all the information we need," she suggested, as he looked on the flat surface for a mouse, his right hand twitching a little with disappointment as it ran, albeit in vain, with a slight circular motion on the worktop.

He opened the packet of paper and began to feed it into the printer, which held it grudgingly.

"Wow, I thought for a minute they wouldn't take A4 paper and we'd need some of that computer paper with the sprocket holes on it."

"Before my time," she mused. "Can you still get that?"

"Not seen it in a while," he confirmed.

Petunia once again addressed the recalcitrant computer with the unforgiving and heavy keys. Even simple tasks took an age and the sticky and spongy keys made her fingers ache. Nevertheless, she continued and soon summoned the report menu, from the watery depths of the green screen; she selected items from it one at a time. He looked over her shoulder, impressed by the speed with which she'd become familiar with the ancient interface. She held the keyboard up trying to decipher what was written on the bits of sticky paper that had been applied next to the function keys. Eventually, after pressing yet more of the keys empirically, the printer was persuaded to print the reports, as they ponderously appeared, from the sedate inner workings of the computer.

Some time later all the reports had been called upon and the information they provided had been printed. He gathered all the printed reports together, placing them on his laptop with some relief.

She kissed him again. Her sunny smile was restored as she came up to him and somehow stretched her arms around his neck. She looked down at the black pumps on her feet. "I think I'll need my Louboutins to be able to reach."

"Now, they would cause a bit of a stir round here," he suggested.

She kissed him as she held on. "Very well then, you get off. I'll let you out, lock the door and then slip out through the front door, which will lock behind me: the cleaners will be some time yet. I'll see you at the car," she confirmed, as he gripped her hand.

One of the cleaners had heard the printer chattering in the office. This was an unusual thing for this time of night. She'd heard very different noises on many nights from Dr Rapace's room and had had to alter the cleaning schedule around this. In all her years, however, she'd never heard a printer whirring for some time after the receptionists had gone home. She carefully moved her vacuum cleaner so as not to make too much noise and hid round the corner from the office in order to hear the conversation between voices she didn't recognise. Such strange and hushed voices only reinforced her view that something wasn't right: but who to tell? She moved away quietly as the computer terminal was closed down and positioned herself to peep through the crack in the office door. She saw a young woman, who she'd never seen before, gather her things and slip quietly through the front door, which immediately locked behind her.

The cleaner realised that, although she'd not seen the young woman before, judging by her attire, she must be a receptionist. New staff were always being taken on; she'd seen so many come and go like cats at a fair. Yet, this one was behaving strangely. Most of the receptionists almost ran through the door as soon as 6pm arrived. At such a time it was as if they were under starter's orders and were simply waiting for the crack of the pistol before they swept through the exit. The cleaner hastily assembled questions within. Just why was she lingering in the office? Who was the man that she had just seen off the premises and why was she running the computer and printers in this way? What did a receptionist need such printouts for? What could she possibly be up to? Who should she tell?

Question after question queued with urgency, but the cleaner hadn't, at this stage, any answers.

Over the next few nights, if the opportunity presented, and she had a feeling it would, then she'd find out. Either that or she'd have to tell someone. This opened the most difficult dilemma of all. Who to confide in? In truth, she knew there was only one person she could trust, and heaven knew he had enough problems.

Petunia closed the door behind her and the latch caught immediately. She wasn't aware of the cleaner watching her round the edge of the office door. Evening wore on and it was growing dark. The outside lights had come on courtesy of their timers, a small strip of car park being illuminated by their somewhat anaemic light. Notwithstanding this, however, as the receptionist looked down she noted clumps of earth on the tarmac deposited like very large dominoes on the baize of a card table. Something had created them and the regular and parallel pattern was both out of place and distinctive. She knew immediately that such tracks appearing here, in this place, was unusual but could not understand who or what had caused them and with what purpose.

The wind caught her and seemed to pass right through her thin blouse. The cold that overran her seemed to exacerbate the gloom and the dampness that hung in the air. She ran from the car park, past Matilda Spencer's cottage, in order to find the little car that awaited her. As the driver opened the passenger door, he pressed the button to start the engine.

Chapter V

Front Page News

The following day, the *Horwich Chronicle* was published. The problems at the West Pennine surgery were featured on the front page just underneath an exposé about a local resident who'd been prosecuted for benefit fraud. He'd claimed a hundred thousand pounds in benefits saying that he could neither walk nor even dress himself. Unfortunately, for him, unwisely, he'd allowed the publication of an article on a social media page featuring him doing an open-water swim across the docks at Salford Quays. His ex-wife had seen the article on his Facebook page and promptly shopped him to the fraud division of the Department for Work and Pensions.

Although the surgery article had been placed below the lead article, what it lacked in prominence it more than made up for in content. The correspondent was crowing about his securing confidential inside information that had been leaked to him by his undisclosed but well-connected source. Casualty attendances and the non-elective admissions (NEL), which were seen as crucial indicators of the performance of a surgery, were dismal. The Government were particularly interested in such figures as they, at a stroke, highlighted failing surgeries, those that were in such disarray that patients had no choice but to rely on Accident and Emergency and the local hospital to see them because the GP surgery either could not or would not. Even worse than this, such cases were often trivial and belonged within the realm of primary care where they could be dealt with both quickly and, perhaps of greater concern to the government, more cheaply.

National press continued to excoriate the government over casualty waiting times, trolley waits and ambulance waits and it was clear that, especially in certain areas, figures were worsening. One prominent and well-known Casualty department had received such bad press over their poor trolley wait times that they had struck upon an imaginative solution. Simply by removing the wheels from the trolleys piling up in casualty and now calling them temporary beds meant a complete re-drawing of the offending figures in a much more favourable light.

The local newspaper correspondent had asked for a statement from the local CCG and also the CCA; both declined to pass any comment. The CCA, or Clinical Commissioning Authority, had been set up to police CCGs that were made up of GPs and other clinicians who were charged with providing a service. In order that fair play and accountability were always to the fore, the CCA kept a close eye on the CCG that, in turn, kept a close eye on individual GP surgeries. The CCA were initially tight-lipped. After being pressed by the reporter, and aware that he seemed to have access to a wealth of highly sensitive data, they did volunteer that each surgery was subject to periodic review and that if any were seen to have failed, after being in the equivalent of special measures, then the inspectors from each agency had the power, the duty and the authority to close such an establishment down with little notice. Although this would only be done as a last resort, both the CCA and CCG were charged with an obligation both to the patients and also to the public purse. They were invested at all times with the responsibility of ensuring that public money was not wasted on so-called failing surgeries. If such evidence ever came to light then patients would be swiftly re-allocated to other GPs in the area.

An unflattering picture of Dr Binder, running to his car in

the middle of a squall was included in the newspaper article and this set the scene for the whole piece that they'd run. Not mentioned, however, was the insistence from the CCA that their comment was a general one that applied to every GP surgery within their area of influence and had been provided with the requirement that they could not and would not comment about specific surgeries. This rider had not only been ignored by the reporter but the inclusion of the unfortunate photo left no one in doubt as to which surgery was in the frame. Dr Binder's unhappy features showed up in even more stark relief against the storm-tossed moorland scene, one which Heathcliff himself would have recognised.

Annabelle arrived at work that same morning, reaching the surgery just before 8:30. She knew that the repeat prescription box had not been emptied from the day before, but she was at least hoping to put a dent in the masses of requests that it would contain. Although she hardly dared to admit it to herself, there was something about the new girl, and her methods, that was compelling, and offered an end, or at least a limit, to the unhappy queues that had become the norm. For that moment in time her brain could picture a happier way of working.

She looked around; the reality of life in the surgery under the cruel ministrations of the practice manager was very different. Her new-found confidence, and optimism, evaporated in the time in which it took her to lift the box. She knew, deep within, that things were unlikely to change and her bright thoughts evaporated. Perhaps it was not good for one to dream.

More shock lay in wait. She looked quickly, almost disbelievingly, inside the box. Horror mounted within. She picked it up, tapped it and rubbed it like a magic lamp but none of these things altered the reality, as she turned it out, that it was quite empty. As she turned it back over she patted it like a magician attempting to summon a rabbit from a hat only for her to see out of the corner of her eye the furry mammal making its bid for freedom. She then could only hope that her eyes had been deceived in some way by the smooth and glossy, but quite empty, interior and she then swept her hand around its inner confines. She wafted it helplessly for a little while like a net hoping that a precious butterfly or, more hopefully, a weighty prescription request or two might materialise inside any moment. Sadly, it was not to be. The gleaming daylight served only to highlight the absolute emptiness of the prescription box, for the first time and as far back as any could remember.

She dropped the box back on its shelf as if it were contaminated in some way and posed a risk to all that might have occasion to touch it. She stared at it. She rubbed the back of her neck as she wondered what she should do. By rights she knew that she, along with all the patients that would make an attempt to collect one of those, now finalised, prescriptions that day, should be delighted. Sadly however, for whatever reason, things that would normally be a relief or a measure of efficiency and delight did not apply at this surgery which was far from normal. As she swallowed with difficulty, her throat tightened as if a noose had been applied. The prescription box was empty and no matter how many times she looked at it, it remained so.

At first a sense of wonder visited her face. Who could have done such a thing? But even before the thought crystallised within her brain the answer had been returned to her. In truth it could only have been one person – the new girl. It was, in turn, to be replaced by unabridged panic as she thought of what would happen when the practice manager found out, as she knew that just about everything that happened in the surgery fell under her razor-like, deliberative gaze.

The older girls had taken Annabelle to one side on more than one occasion and advised her not to get herself noticed. 'Just turn up, do the minimum and then go home and do not care about anyone or anything else, least of all the patients', was the mantra – one that assured survival. That's the way it was and anyone who thought differently had been confronted in front of the whole surgery and patients too, and told that they no longer fitted in with the ethos of the surgery and what Dr Binder was hoping to achieve. They had shaken their heads, their faces white with fear, as they told their tales with quavering voices through gritted teeth. Under no circumstances, make any attempt, any attempt whatsoever, to better the lot of the patients.

For sure, she'd seen with her own eyes what happened in pretty short order to those who'd dared to use initiative; to take some vestige of pride in their work, and those who tried to go up against the manager – or to think that others would save them when common sense prevailed. Truth is, nobody came to their rescue, ever, and their protest, if that's how it could be described, was over long before the words from the manager hit them – like a lorry driven directly at them by a mad woman and with similar obliterative effect. Before they'd had a chance to draw breath, they would begin the long walk up to the main road, to catch the next bus that came along. Their heads would be in a whirl, not knowing quite what had befallen them.

Ms Makepeace would stride around the office, her hands on her ample hips, like a captain, with unassailable authority and confidence, in a ship full of pressed and doomed sailors. It was painfully true that invariably after such an event they were not seen again.

Annabelle accepted that she'd be in the firing line as soon as that empty box was detected. She knew only that she could not afford to lose her job and that locally employment prospects were poor. This single fact, unfortunately, allowed the manager to wield power that cut far more effectively than the cat, brought to bear on terrified men's backs. Annabelle decided in that moment that the wise move was needed here, the one that would hopefully assure her safety and longevity in the high attrition practice. At its simplest this would mean allowing the box to fill up again and doing the bare minimum to keep up the semblance of being busy which was just how the manager wanted it. She wondered if she had time to create a few requests herself and pop them in the box.

It seemed like a distant memory or even a waking dream just how good it had felt for those few seconds. The saddest thing was that Annabelle had forgotten just how rewarding it was, seeing the patients' eyes light up when their pretty low expectations were met or even exceeded. The sheer delight when a request was actioned or had even been anticipated was compelling with almost an addictive quality. This was the buzz of success; of working as a team, of having pride in one's work; one's job and being part of something that was much greater than the sum of its humble parts. Receiving thanks from grateful patients was also wonderful and though it was a new experience, the young receptionist had basked in the warm glow that was generated when such words were received. Like most folk the receptionists always felt better with positive sentiments, rather than the customary negative ones.

Annabelle would have rather less time than she thought to consider the delight that accompanied the efficient service that just a few changes could create. She wouldn't even have time to throw a few dummy requests in the box; for catastrophe was a second away and it was heading straight for her. Amanda Makepeace had seen the young receptionist tip the box out in this way. Her conclusions appeared like an avalanche covering an unwary skier.

She approached the doomed girl, as might a shark moving in for a swift and brutal kill.

The others started with horror, knowing what was about to befall the unwary receptionist, who was now stalled in time. They knew, too, that she needed her job, as did they, and also she'd be unlikely to find another. The first hint that Annabelle received that her days in the surgery, and her job, were about to draw to a precipitous close came from the vibration that registered the heavy footfalls transmitted by the insubstantial floor as the manager closed on her. Annabelle didn't dare turn round, for she knew who would be standing there and what would happen next; her neck prickled with alarm. The manager did not wait for her to speak.

"Who's cleared the box? I've told you all that the doctors prefer the prescription requests to build up in order to keep costs down. If patients obtain their items too soon or too quickly then this pushes through into prescription costs for the doctors and the prescribing budget is already overflowing with red ink as it is. Prescription costs *must* be kept down if we are to survive. I can see despite my *clear* instructions, you have taken matters out of my hands. Was it you who has emptied the box in this way?" Without doubt, Amanda Makepeace knew that the question was unanswerable. It was rather like accusing someone of being a witch. Any given answer would assure their condemnation and the need to dunk them in the nearest available deep river. She could see the receptionist begin to squirm like a worm being caught on a hot concrete flag on a sun-baked day. The hapless girl looked from side to side but knew in that moment that nothing and no one could, or would, save her. Amanda knew it was time to turn the heat up another notch. She glared at the girl, her blue-grey eyes boring into her like laser beams about to split atoms.

Ten people in the office held their breath, none daring to move let alone respire. Only the manager seemed at comfort, now in her natural element, and the more unpleasant it got the more she revelled in it. Annabelle was certain that she licked her lips.

There was a slight pause, a hiatus in the timeline, where a moment of unrestrained horror flourished and all who gave witness would be compelled to revisit it just as they had on the last occasion and the one before that. Amanda made ready for the kill – the bit she liked best of all.

One person shattered the brutal gap and time continued at least for all the others, now released, as the culprit stood. They knew that even before she spoke she would occupy the spotlight that would now fall on the damned. The girls had warned her on several occasions and now she was to pay the same price, as had so many of her predecessors. Susan couldn't help but nod. Not that she took any delight whatsoever in the almost ritual slaughter of yet another innocent but she was clear in her own mind that she'd done her duty and warned the newcomer of the errors of her ways. Sadly, the new girl was about to experience for herself what the more experienced receptionists had tried to warn her about. At least she was going to own up and not let another pay the price of her rash stupidity.

"It was me who cleared the box. My bus was early and I thought I was helping out. I am so sorry," Petunia offered, cautiously. Her mind was barely able to encompass what her eyes and ears told her was happening. Surely, in just about every surgery, what she'd done was a good thing. She could see now what the girls had warned her against and its full effect was about to obliterate her as the manager's gaze traversed round like the turret in a tank about to open fire. For this, clearly, was neither a typical nor normal surgery. It was almost as if she'd slipped through some space and time continuum where rational rules no longer applied. She gulped and tried to swallow as her throat closed off. Her words seemed trapped in the ether; pleasant and honest enough to surely dispel the harsh thought from just about any reasonable and caring person. Sadly, the practice manager eschewed both of these attributes.

The other receptionists doubted that her naivety would save her. Ignorance had hitherto never been accepted as an excuse. As they thought more about it, they realised that *nothing* was accepted as an excuse: any moment Petunia would be making the long walk with the cardboard box full of a few meagre effects. The manager was unable to repress the smile, bordering on sheer relief, that visited her face with its sharp features. Now she did lick her lips for sure. This outcome was beyond her wildest dreams. She'd been suspicious of the new girl and her abilities that seemed oddly disconnected from her physical appearance and demeanour. Such things she could neither risk nor tolerate when her plans were so far advanced. Good fortune smiled upon her just when she needed it. Now had come her opportunity and she smiled as might a crocodile about to entrap its hapless prey. The teeth became more visible just before the feast.

In that moment, just before she could speak, however, another event intruded upon them. Dr Binder walked through the reception. Nobody had noticed him, or his quiet flat walk as he came in. The sadness that accompanied him like a tightly-wrapped scarf around his neck was fleetingly loosened. He hadn't heard much but he sensed the withering environment within the office and he caught Amanda glance at the empty prescription boxes that more than one of the girls had used to collect their things.

"I'll deal with this Ms Makepeace. Please come down to my office, Miss Mumple."

Absolute hush remained in force. This was outweighed to a significant extent by the weight of stares, focussed like a beam that would split stone, directed towards the GP and the new girl as he led the way from the office. Incredulity had temporarily stunned them all. So many mouths remained open as if the shock had precluded their closure.

Even the practice manager stared, but her visage was modulated more by suspicion and anger than any other emotion. She looked around the office and the spell of stasis was broken. The girls quickly busied themselves, not wanting to be subjected to the lash of her disappointment at having her next dismissal elude her. A single unifying thought ran through every mind: Dr Binder was always nice with every single one of them, but he'd never been known to intervene before and had simply allowed the manager to practise her reign of abuse on any who came within her arc of fire. They couldn't believe that he was so duplicitous as to be simply asking the manager to do his dirty work. All held the view that he was either unaware of her practices or was so dependent on her skills to keep him, as she claimed at every verse end, out of the clutches of the surgery inspectors from the CCG. Most had concluded long ago that it was due to both of these things.

Her parting shot was delivered with more acidity than even her habitual tones, "Very well then, Doctor, if you don't wish me to deal with the matter."

Petunia followed him docilely down the dank and dark corridor to his room, her slacks rubbing along the linoleum-covered floor that had long since been worn to a smooth, thin and shiny finish.

"Sit down, Petunia, please," he added almost as an afterthought as the events took him by surprise.

He closed the thin plywood-panelled door, which was stained in a colour almost the same shade as the pine cladding which had aged to a burnt-treacle colour.

"I am not sure what to believe here, Petunia. I wonder if you could clarify for me what I heard as I came through reception just now? I was given to understand that the girls were so overworked, and so few in number, that there isn't time for them in a day to clear the box. Apparently, we have so much trouble recruiting staff either in sufficient numbers or of sufficient quality, or both, as to make even the routine stuff impossible to complete. What have you to say about that, Petunia?"

She paused, but this unusual event existed only for the briefest interval. He could see the smile flourish as she considered herself happy with the reply that had formed.

"Dr Binder, I think you have some wonderful staff; perhaps it's simply that they need a bit of confidence and, shall I say, a bit of encouragement – a few positive strokes in their direction? I came in early, Dr Binder, just to help out. I didn't realise it would be a problem."

His smile vanished like a shimmer of autumnal light on a butterfly's wing. The sadness that weighed him down like a wet blanket on a horse's back, re-established itself. However, on this occasion an iota of curiosity was strong enough to flicker on his face.

"Something has changed here and it's happened recently. Since you came, I believe. Petunia, who are you?"

"I'm just the new girl, Dr Binder."

"Why do I keep thinking you are a bit more than that, maybe a lot more than that?

Even beneath the untidy fringe he became aware of the dazzling smile appearing like the sun on a misty day with a promise of routing the haze and replacing it with life-giving warmth, a catalyst that would fuel every positive reaction that life was capable of experiencing.

Petunia looked at the silver-framed photo on his desk; she could not help but notice the wedding ring that appeared not to have been separated from his left hand for many years. After a short but palpable pause, he began again.

"Please tell me?"

"As I said, I'm just the new girl."

Words having failed, he then used silence and a penetrating stare, one normally reserved for a being vacating an alien spacecraft, to persuade her of his need to learn just a little more than he detected she was willing to reveal.

She nodded, acknowledging his mounting discomfort. She looked again at the wedding ring, having been told that he wasn't married: yet all the signs that lay before her were of someone very much in the throes of marriage, and perhaps unhappily so. Notwithstanding this, what was clear was the unremitting sadness, ever present, that encircled him like a walled city in a permanent state of siege. He looked so unhappy at this moment that she knew she had to offer a means of at least checking his descent into more misery than she could bear to witness.

She smiled, once again. She took a deep breath in. "I am just a friend, Dr Binder, who means you no harm. Forgive me, but you are not quite ready to learn why I am here. I wonder if I might ask for your indulgence and, if it were possible, for you to prevent Ms Makepeace from dismissing me, as I suspect you did today?"

"Dismiss you! Why should she do that? When you are clearly exactly the sort of person my surgery needs."

"I hope I don't sound offensive if I tell you that there are many things going on behind your back that you have yet to discover. If perhaps you could simply accept the possibility that this may be so, then I'll do my best with the remainder."

Looking more stunned than upset or angry, he mouthed the words 'who are you?', but more to himself as she turned to go, the enigmatic smile seeming to linger like an apparition in the ether even after its source had departed. She passed quietly through the door, only the faint hint of bright, fragrant perfume still lingering when she'd done so.

He sat for several minutes, tortured and tantalised in equal measure by the words she'd obviously chosen with care. He looked forlornly at the photo on his desk. The new girl had seen right through him and, perhaps, what she saw was not palatable. She'd hinted politely that he'd been asleep at the helm for too long. Only then did his mind move on to thoughts as to what might have happened during this time to a crew desperate to prove that they could be hard working as well as loyal. Moreover, many of the words spoken by Tina, the day she departed, came back to visit him in that moment as he accepted, at last, that there may well be some truth in what both receptionists were trying to tell him. In that moment a single conclusion formed. Rising to his feet, he went to find the practice manager, in her room.

"I've spoken to the new girl. I don't think she'd grasped the way in which we do things here and I've asked her to do her best to fit in more with the other girls here at the surgery. She tells me that she's sorry if it looks like she's been rocking the boat."

Amanda Makepeace looked carefully at the senior doctor. She could swear she could see a hint of good old-fashioned gumption. Shame it was coming too late to save him, or his surgery. "Very well, Doctor, I defer as always to your good offices. Thank you for letting me know. I suspect that the receptionist in question represents far more trouble than you or I should wish to accept, but for now I will reserve any further comment until a future date." The look that she gave him at this point caused more questions and doubts to crystallise within the mind of the senior partner, her employer.

She stared for a little while even after he had withdrawn from her room. For the first time, a flicker of admiration for him crossed her mind; sad to say it was far too late and the fate that was about to befall him was entirely of his own making.

Furthermore, it would take a far more clever and devious person to even attempt to pull the wool over her eyes. She made her mind up there and then that Petunia would be history before the week was out.

Most vitally, she had thought that, in Miss Mumple, she'd taken on a fool. The CV and the references confirmed this to be the case, but she now knew that there was a very different person in their midst than indicated by her file – someone, perhaps, who was not all she seemed. That made two of them: it took one to know one. Amanda wondered just how might such a person come to arrive in a little surgery like this of no account and how could she possibly have discovered the real game that was in play. In any event a little checking up on their new receptionist would do no harm and was probably now overdue. She pulled Petunia's file and scrutinised it line by line. A frisson of something she despised ran down her spine and she recognised it, with a shiver, for what it was – simple fear. Mercifully, her plans were rapidly coming to fruition and it was very unlikely that some untidy receptionist, whatever her true motives, could stop her now.

CHAPTER VI

Intruder

Evening found Petunia alone in the office. She had told the other girls to go ahead of her and she would run up to the bus stop in a little while, having one or two things to tidy. They looked at one another a little worriedly as she said this as they wondered if, come the morning, she or they would have to fend off another attack from their fear-provoking manager. As soon as she could be sure they had all departed, she unlocked the side entrance and a short time later she heard a light tapping sound. She opened the reinforced steel door, revealing the tall man standing in the deepening darkness. She kissed him enthusiastically.

"Someone's been making enquiries about you today. It's a good job that you were placed here by a proper medical staffing agency, and not some fly-by-night company."

"I told you that we should do it properly," she murmured thoughtfully.

"And my love, right you were, to suggest such a thing. Anyway, I gave Ms Makepeace the names of some of your referees and no doubt she phoned them, too. She seemed really keen to check you out, so you must have rattled her. Hopefully she won't be any the wiser once she's made her enquiries."

"Just be careful, she's no fool."

"Anyway, I just need one or two reports off the computer and then I should have an idea as to what you've got yourself into." Petunia stood in front of the ageing computer as a pianist might in front of an antique instrument. This keyboard, however, was much more uncooperative and, without doubt, worth rather less.

Nimble fingers thumped a little against the reluctant keys as she attempted to press them into life with a little, sticky crackle. Half an hour later he picked up the paper from the printer. He brought the pages together carefully and made towards the side entrance so that she could let him out. It was then that Petunia noticed that they were not alone. Emma Sparkle, senior cleaner, stood in the entrance to the office.

"Saw you two the other night, just what kind of skul.., skul…, skulduggery are you two up to?"

Her left hand was on her hip; with the other she carried a mop, a little awkwardly like a soldier expected to do drill without a rifle.

"You're up to no good, I'm guessin'," she declared, as her eyes narrowed and her head nodded having, without a doubt, confirmed what she already knew. "I'm not quite sure whether to go to Ms Makepeace, the police, the papers, or Dr Binder. Who would you suggest?"

Petunia had given a little start when she noticed the cleaner standing there, looking a little agitated. Her calm melodic words came forth as she looked unwaveringly at the unexpected visitor. More than this, it was the charming smile that reassured the other woman.

"Of those options, then I'd prefer Dr Binder, please. It's Emma isn't it, I'm Petunia." She then held out her hand causing Emma to put down her mop.

Though her features remained impassive, the receptionist had provided her with a good answer: one that reassured.

"Okay, so why him and just what do you think I should be tellin' him? That one of his receptionists is printing stuff off the computer. No doubt confidential reports, and givin' 'em to another stranger who takes 'em away with 'im before she then leaves. Is it you sellin' the surgery out to that newspaper man?"

"Yes, you could tell him exactly that, but please don't forget to say that I mean him no harm. In point of fact, I am here to help him. And no, it isn't me who's leaking to the newspapers."

Despite the intense scrutiny under which Emma placed the receptionist, she detected no fear, no subterfuge and no hidden corners; just an open manner – which itself, was only partially obscured by the unruly fringe. Moreover, she couldn't help but agree that the poor soul, Dr Binder, needed something and help would be a good start, though her steely expression did its best to conceal such a thought. More significantly, curiosity had by now displaced suspicion in the cleaner's mind. It was also true that the leaks had been appearing in the *Chronicle* for many months before the new girl had started.

"So, how do you know Dr Binder?"

"I don't."

"What are you doing here, then?"

"I'm here to help him."

Emma was by now even more intrigued. "Why, if you don't know him?"

"I was sent a letter, asking for help."

"A letter!"

"A letter."

"A letter, and you just pitched up?"

"It seemed the right thing to do," the young couple nodded at her in unison.

With these words the cleaner laughed, her face betraying her incredulity, "Why? These days folk don't give two hoots, whether someone's strugglin' or otherwise, they pass on by."

"Because, I'm told that he's a kind, gentle man, a good doctor who's served his patients here diligently until very recently."

"That he has."

"But who sent it?" She asked again as the puzzle on her face refused to be extinguished.

"I don't know."

"A letter an' you don't know who from?" She laughed again, but curiosity was now firmly in charge.

"No, that's true. It could be anyone, was it you?"

"No girlie it wan't me. So, you've no idea who sent it?"

"Correct."

"Somethin's tellin' me you ain't the brightest bulb on the Christmas tree, eh girlie."

"I never said I was, but at least I'm here, and I'm doing my best!"

"No offence, eh girlie. Right enough, that you are, though you are only a young un. You 'n all," she nodded to the tall, handsome man.

The cleaner paused again; so many questions queued within her mind but she had become fascinated by the young receptionist, who clearly wasn't really a receptionist at all. "So, letter or no letter, why should it bother you?"

"I couldn't ignore the heart-rending tale of how much this place has crashed."

"Not surprising, given what's gone on. I still can't see why that should be your concern."

"Emma, please take a look around. What do you see?"

Despite her knowing every inch of the building she did as she was asked. After a pause she replied, "I see a surgery that's fadin' fast. No, one that's already dead on its feet. It's just that nobody has told it to lie down and die quietly."

"Why is that, do you think?" she asked the older woman to clarify.

"They are here, all of them, just for one man. Someone who is the absolutist kindest, most magnificent doctor ever to grace the West Pennine moors. He's been so kind to me and my Bill, at least before he upped and died with his lung cancer. Came every week he did, without fail."

"Sorry to hear that, Emma."

"Few years ago now, before he was distracted by the accident."

"Who, your Bill?"

"Na, silly, Dr Binder!" She focussed her eyes, which were now alight. "Say, y'don't know do ya girlie?"

"Know what?"

"About the accident! She's 'ad letter but don't know what 'appened!" she said more to herself than them.

Her reply came by way of a gentle shake of her head: the cascade of hair describing the same rhythm as she did so.

"Destroyed him, it did. Five years now have passed, but you can tell he lives it as if it's only just happened. He lives every second of it, be sure he does. The grief that'll never die. That's what they say and they're all right. His wife and the most beautiful little boy ya did ever see."

"So *what* happened?" She asked with a little impatience creeping in. Petunia's eyes now widened like two pools of the most perfect hue of cerulean appearing in the sky on a summer's day.

"His wife went down to the shops one night. It'd been raining and they put one of them fancy pavements in that juts out in the road. She hit this an' broke two tyres and wheels. She was fine, but the car 'ad to be brought back on one o' them transporters. She couldn't drive it so he ordered two new tyres and wheels from the garage. Apparently, they gave 'im fancy new tyres, could only be used one way round. Directional, they said, or at least, the papers said afterwards, like. But they gave him two for the *wrong* side. Course, he fitted 'em and didn't realise they were the wrong uns. The ones for the inside should'a gone on the outside. Silly fools, them weren't the ones damaged."

She paused to make sure that the younger woman was still with her. Petunia nodded by way of confirmation but she didn't speak as she sensed already the disaster that had engulfed the then young GP.

"He didn't check for sure, only they didn't ask – if ya see? Didn't check if they'd given 'im correct uns."

Petunia nodded again but with mounting concern. She had the feeling that another piece of the jigsaw was about to be put in position – and tragically so.

"Anyways, he fits these new tyres. Thinks no more about it. One Saturday it were rainin' cats 'n' dogs and she drove, just her and the littl'un over to her mum's, over yonder Blackburn way. Took the old road past the disused quarry. There were a lot of water on the road. It were a tight bend and they say she took it a bit fast and off the road they came, car 'n' everything. Both were killed outright, should'a seen the car when they pulled it outa that quarry, put a concrete fence there now, but too late to save 'em." A little tear formed in the receptionist's eyes as they reflected the heartbreak that had visited that young family that day.

Emma's voice dropped a register and she began whispering as she now drifted into ground that was more hearsay, but had clearly been widely circulated. "They say she were perched on the edge, couldn't get out. Little car was lashed by that storm on that cold, wet night. They say she phoned 'im for 'elp an all 'e 'eard was screams as the car went over th'edge."

She paused as she detected the look of mounting horror and distress on the young woman's face.

"You didn't know anything of this did ya?"

Petunia shook her head, not sure that she'd be able to speak in that moment. She did her best to wipe away the tears but the more she tried the more they appeared. Emma reached into the deep pockets of her smock and produced a tissue that passed for being clean although Petunia noted that it smelt of furniture polish. The tall man, too, was gripped but also profoundly saddened.

"Some say 'e died that day, too. I think they're right. For sure, he only blamed hisself. That little boy was so handsome. She used to bring 'im 'ere. Some say he was like an angel, needed in 'eaven. I couldn't argue miself, for sure he was absolutely beautiful. Anyways e's up there now with 'is mam. Only, Dr Binder went to hell that day and e's still there."

She paused a little, her voice becoming deeper still as if she were now imparting something known only to a few. "They say th'insurance took the garage ta court and he were awarded a few hundred thousand. He wunt take a penny so I'm told. He said it was all 'is own fault.

Apparently, there was a big arrow on the side of the tyre. Who'd ever heard of a tyre being the wrong way round. A tyre is a tyre, yes?"

"I'd have thought so," Petunia agreed with a little nod as she struggled a little less with her tears but more with a very soggy tissue that now smelt of wet furniture polish.

"Anyways, for sure, whatever the truth, he only blamed hisself. As I say, they say he died that day, and what's left is just a shell. Hollow and empty, like an egg wi no yolk. Him, bein' such a kind man the local folk stayed loyal to him though, as yer can see, his surgery went to rack and ruin. He was so good to my Bill, nothin' too much trouble, before he died. When he died I was so hard up he said I could have this job here and he was as true as his word. Fat lot of good it did me, the mortgage company say I'm so far behind on the payments they are still gonna fore.., fore.., take mi house off me. Not that it's his fault, of course, I couldn'a had a better GP, for sure. Nor better employer. There's a lovely grave in Horwich cemetery. They say little un's buried in his mam's arms. They say there's a space there for him, and he won't be long claimin' it. That's why this place is like it is, specially since *she* came twelve months ago. But I 'ad a feelin' you knew that bit didn't ya? Am I right, Miss?"

Petunia coughed back the tears in her throat. "Amanda Makepeace, you mean?" Emma nodded, "Yes, I was told about her in the letter."

"They call 'er Missolini." Petunia laughed as the tears finally stopped.

"So back to you, Miss, and you handsome fella. Just what are you two doin' here in the middle of nowhere?"

"We are going to do our best to help him and the surgery," answered the tall, handsome man who had also been stunned by the tragedy behind the cleaner's tale and had only now managed to recover his voice.

Emma just had to return to the piece of information that tantalised her most. "So ya get a letter, from someone you don't know and 'ere you are?"

"Yes, that's about it."

"Well, good luck to you girlie. And you, too, handsome," she nodded to the tall man who was still clutching his sheets of paper. "You'll need it with her around. They say no one can stand up to her. What good can you do, forgive me like, just you and him that's left to go up against her? You don't seem sophisticated types, beggin' yer pardon."

"No, but I am going to try to help him, Dr Binder, I mean."

"Don't think you'll do much but what do I know."

"It won't be for want of trying, Emma."

"Yes, I can see that in yer like, Miss. Well good luck, Miss. At least for the moment I won't be breathin' a word of what I've seen, to no-one like.

Just be careful against her; anyone who takes her on leaves and is never seen again like.

So girlie don't say I didn't warn yer. Anyone who goes up in the ring against her wishes they hadn't unless they can run well, I tell ya. I don't know what he's doin with her," she pointed to Dr Rapace's door, "should hear what she does to him when they're here alone. Shocks me it does! Me being a widowed woman and all." She then moved towards the flimsy double doors.

Emma let Petunia and the tall chap, who hastily grabbed his laptop, out through the door. They thanked her but both were deep in thought, so much so that for the moment neither could form words. The only crumb of comfort was that at least a little more of the puzzle had fallen into place.

As they stepped out into yet another wind-torn night, Petunia looked around for the little car that she knew would be nearby. As she looked, however, she noticed, once again, the track marks set in mud in a rigid pattern. She looked along their direction of travel. There in the distance she thought she caught the brief appearance of a bright light. Curiosity fired within. He led the way towards the little car, parked just off the road and in the shadows so that it was not easy to spot unless one knew that it was there. At first, she walked over, and placed a hand on the passenger door, but continued to look back at where she thought she'd seen the flash of light. Just as she did so she saw another flash of bright, white light and then, after a second or two, another.

The tall man held her hand, sensing her distraction. "Come on, I'm starving and dying for a pee, let's go."

"No, hold on a moment, there's something back there. Look down at these marks; I saw them the other night. I think these marks are tracks and whatever has made them is over there. Can you wait?"

"You'll be ages, I'm dying for a pee. What could possibly be going on over there? It's completely deserted moorland and it looks pretty chilly and uninviting, I might add."

"Sorry, my love, but this is very strange, it's *all* very strange and now is a good time to find out. I am guessing the clues will be absent in the daytime. I need to look now and to check on this. If it's nothing then I'll come running back, I promise. I think there's something going on," she pointed back the way she had come, "and it's right over there, if I am not mistaken. Can you hold on? You could always go behind that nice little bush over there." He looked somewhat reluctantly at the indicated bush and in that moment his bladder calmed somewhat. She smiled, sensing that he was more comfortable. "Stay here and I won't be long, but get ready to start the engine in case we need to leave in a hurry."

"What! It sounds like you are going to rob a bank!" he exclaimed, getting into the car but shifting uneasily on his seat as his bladder reminded him he'd been given the most temporary of reprieves.

"You are not going to pull a stocking over your head are you?"

She looked at him and angled her head a little, "Now, you

are getting giddy on me," she said, as she smiled at him affectionately.

"Yes, and it's also known as advanced starvation and bladder explosion if you are not quick."

"I'll be as quick as I can." She leaned over to kiss him lightly.

He was about to tell her that it was unlikely he'd be able to hang on for much longer, but she'd already closed the door before he could say more. He looked again at the little bush which looked uninviting and also very prickly. Even within the car he could feel the gusts of the cold wind. She walked along the direction of the regular and geometric shapes of earth that had been laid down on the tarmac of the surgery car park and extended way past it.

Despite the surgery lights still being on, it remained very dark in the car park and initially she crouched a little until her steps seemed to be more secure. She picked up her pace and now walked more quickly and stealthily as she followed the tracks as they led down and away from the main road and past the surgery. The ground here was rough but at least covered in long grass and some heather. She noted despite the dark that much of it had been broken up and the same tracked pattern had been embossed upon it.

What was not in darkness, however, was the skyline. Every once in a while, a bright light seemed to be emanating from over the crest of the steep slope that lay beyond the surgery car park. The appearance resembled a vast electrical storm, which was still over the horizon.

She was able to make out the hills which stretched either side of the pathway she had elected to follow, their steep slopes rose up on either side of her direction of travel. The bright light seemed to be more easily defined as she continued; it illuminated the gap between the crest of the slope and the distant horizon. She continued to walk for some time, at all times following the bursts of bright light on the ever-approaching horizon.

Then, she noticed the noise. The wind had masked it almost completely. She looked carefully in the available light at her watch. 10pm, surely the time an elderly lady might turn in.

The steepness of the slope increased and her shoes fought desperately for grip; but thirst for information was by now firmly in charge of all other considerations. She kept on going.

After some time she reached the top of the hill. At this point she was rewarded with discovery, which effectively displaced any surprise. More vitally came knowledge, for she now understood both the reason why a little old lady was hearing noises in the night and also the source of the marks in the car park. She wondered, too, if she'd found the real reason as to why the surgery was in such danger. Her discovery had been shrouded in a wall of blackout sheeting, put there to hide what lay beyond from prying eyes. The edge of one of the sheets had worked loose and the wind was responsible for causing a large corner of the sheet to rise up, thereby allowing the escape of light every few seconds and also allowing Petunia to glimpse what lay beyond.

All the clues now lay before her and her acute and inventive mind lost no time in deciphering the importance of such clues. She reasoned that she'd need an expert opinion to make sure that her intuition was correct. Taking a gold iPhone out of her pocket, she took pictures and a short video of the scene that stretched in front of her. She'd seen enough and knew that his full bladder and empty stomach would be unwilling to wait much longer. With mounting excitement, she retraced her route and made for the little car, which still waited for her.

"C'mon, I'm dying for a pee here!"

"Well, at least you are pleased to see me. I told you there is a nice bush over there."

"It would be just my luck to get arrested for some public order offence. Or to get spiked in the unmentionables by that prickly bush."

"I don't think there are many police hiding in scrubby

bushes on deserted moorland at this time of night."

"Ha! So, then, Miss *Mumple*, leaving my bladder to one side for the moment, just what, may I ask, are *we* doing here?"

"We are finding stuff out."

"Well, have we discovered anything other than the odd sheep who's had their sleep interrupted or whatever sheep do to interrupt at night while I am dying here of a burst bladder?"

He shifted uncomfortably in the driver's seat and was about to press the round button to start the car.

Suddenly, she noticed that the cleaners had left the surgery and were now walking up the long lane to the bus stop at the top and past Mrs Spencer's house.

"Okay, it's only the cleaners leaving, let's get going shall we?"

"Oh, at last."

He pressed the 'start' button and the car fired immediately. He revved the engine, going just a little too fast. "And you'll be getting points on your licence in a minute," she offered mischievously.

He shifted with more discomfort and groaned with the agonies that only a full bladder and a cold night could bring.

"I just hope it was worth it. Did you find anything?"

"Oh yes. I'm not one hundred per cent sure just what I've seen but I think it's crucial and explains an awful lot. I am sure while I am at work tomorrow, earning an honest crust, you could take a look at these photos and the short video on my I-phone. I feel sure that this is linked to the surgery in some way. Perhaps send them off to an expert in the industry to see if they know what's going on? I suspect, too, that they are confining their activities to the dead of night and are hoping to keep the number of prying eyes to a minimum."

"Ha! It's a good job they didn't reckon on you being here, then," he said merrily.

For a while her animated talk and excitement distracted him from the pressure and irritation building in his bladder.

"Once you've had a chance to scrutinise the pictures and video, and have had them looked over, I am sure we'll soon have more answers. I have a feeling in my water that this is the key that unlocks this puzzle."

"Just don't mention your water." He said, as she smiled despite the darkness in the car and nodded knowingly in his direction.

Both knew in this day and age that very little could be hidden for more than the most temporary of intervals. The information she'd gleaned would explain the role of at least one person and probably a good many more. The little car sped off, driven a little erratically under the influence of a full bladder.

CHAPTER VII

Dismissal

Disaster struck a few days later. Perhaps Petunia had thought she'd made herself safe, perhaps she'd thought she could depend on Dr Binder to protect her. More prosaically perhaps she'd underestimated Amanda Makepeace's ability to remove anyone she thought might be a problem, or indeed the depths to which she could sink in order to do so. Petunia arrived on time the following day. The practice manager seemed a little more pleasant than usual, but this fact alone should have raised suspicions within the new girl. She began her morning uneventfully enough on the repeat prescription counter. As the morning surgeries started to quieten, she was asked to go into the filing room.

Petunia had cleared the filing a day or two before but, rather like painting a vast metal bridge, it was one of those jobs that never really ceased and a few new letters and items for filing had been placed in the metal tray. Within an hour she had cleared these and she noticed that there were one or two letters in the bottom of the filing tray. She noticed a sealed envelope that was marked 'strictly private and confidential'. Seeing that it was in the filing tray and that it was stamped 'Filing', in black ink, she assumed that it was for filing. She slit open the envelope as she'd done with hundreds of other letters over the preceding few days. Upon withdrawing the paper from the envelope, she saw at once that it contained very sensitive information about the prescribing report for the whole surgery.

Doctors were assessed not only on the cost of the drugs they prescribed but also on certain criteria. These key indicators were also known as performance categories and some of these were linked to accepted modern evidence of good practice. An example of this was the number of antibiotics that a GP prescribed and also the type, as some were widely known to cause problems with resistance and terrible bowel infections that the elderly, in particular, were prone to. There were many other categories that were also carefully assessed. With regard to these, few were in any doubt that they'd been included simply because such drugs were expensive and the government were especially keen to drive down expenditure on those items. Surgeries were therefore placed in green, amber or red zones depending on the volume of such prescriptions.

Petunia couldn't help but notice that the surgery was mostly in the red zone in each of these areas. She decided to simply place the papers back in the envelope and then made sure that the envelope was placed in the practice manager's pigeon hole so that she could deal discreetly with the contents in her own time.

Having finished the filing, she knew that the girls were short on the repeat prescription counter, so she moved back to the office in order to man this station. She had learned by now to quietly regulate provision of the repeat prescriptions and carefully allowed a small queue to build up whenever the manager was present. As soon as the manager had retired to her room, however, the queue went down, and so did the contents of the box as Petunia had now gained considerable expertise with the old and unfamiliar computer system.

The postman came with a large sack and Petunia knew this would create more filing. She was about to return to the filing room and made sure that the prescription box still contained some requests. She looked round as she sensed a commotion. No sooner had she done so, however, when she saw that the girls were also looking round, fear filling each of their expressions, for striding in with very heavy footfalls on substantial black patent stilettos was the office manager. Even those who were turned away were aware of her impending arrival courtesy of the noise her strides made on the linoleum floor. As she arrived in the office Petunia was aware that the manager was wafting a letter agitatedly and without doubt, her face brimming with unrestrained anger. The receptionist soon realised that it was the confidential letter she'd found and opened in the filing room. Notably, the stamped envelope was now missing.

No niceties were observed; the manager allowed her anger and the harsh tone behind her words to flow unequivocally.

"Who has opened this highly confidential letter?" Her words beating a complementary rhythm with the letter as she shook it as one might a raised club. "It's been opened, the contents extracted and, no doubt, read, and then quietly placed in my pigeon hole. It must have arrived at the surgery this morning. What happened to the post?"

One of the girls, Karen, volunteered that she'd taken all the post to the filing room. She hadn't seen the envelope in question but it might have been within the bundle of post. Karen then blushed profusely, her pale features standing out even in the dingy light to be found in reception.

Amanda glared at her with the inquisition that was really being prepared for another.

"Did you open it?" she thundered.

Karen swallowed as if a noose was tightening around her neck. Her face had now taken on a livid hue that spread over her skin. The pale girl, who was now aglow as her heart thundered explosively, nearly fainted under the accusatory manner of the manager who seemed even taller when in such a mood.

"No, not me Ms Makepeace, I only dropped the filing in there."

"Very well then, who has been in filing today?"

Necks and eyes froze, as all present were terrified of laying the finger of suspicion on anyone else. Most of the receptionists looked down at the floor at this point, being incapable of meeting the eye of the explosively unhappy and belligerent manager. They all knew that someone would be making the long walk of dismissal and it looked as though it was to be the new girl who had flown too close to the sun and was about to fall to a painful death on the barren and lonely earth.

Petunia was about to play her final act in what she now realised was all part of the manager's brutal, if not particularly subtle, scheme. As the emotional charge reached even greater heights, time seemed to slow down. Petunia knew in that moment that she'd failed. Failed the GP, the staff and, in addition, the patients who had received the shortest of glimpses of how things used to be. She could only wonder, and not for the first time, who might have sent her the letter and now whether she would ever know, given the fate that was rushing to meet her.

Ms Makepeace raised a sharp and long finger menacingly and she almost managed to suppress the smile of delight from appearing on her face. All too slowly, but mercilessly, the finger was moved round the room like a detective about to identify the culprit who had committed the heinous crime: pointing at each in turn until it rested on the one who was now beyond salvation.

Dark eyes narrowed in on Petunia as they followed the same axis as the damning finger which was now pointing directly towards her.

"Is it you? Have you been in filing this morning, my girl? Have you opened this letter and looked at its confidential contents, because if you have then I am afraid it's instant dismissal."

Not quite content with securing her long awaited opportunity, she now sought to gloat, hesitating a little so as to do so. None of the girls could watch. She turned as if addressing an arena with a fallen gladiator at her feet, one who was now bowed and bloody if not in an even worse state. She even looked up a little as if she were addressing a despotic ruler keen to see blood flow that day.

Amanda continued declaiming to the whole room including many of the patients who could hear from the waiting room. "Some people think they can come here and it does not matter whether they fall in with us or not. Perhaps it's because they think they are better than us that they do as they please." She turned slowly, like an expert bowman with his prey now in his sights, as she spoke the words so that the whole office and a good many of the patients could now hear her booming voice. "Such people need to learn that there is only one outcome for them and it's on the other side of that door."

She wafted an unconcerned hand in the direction of the main door. She looked sharply at Petunia, her words slowing in that moment and finally being charged with more menace than theatre. "I am afraid it's time for us to part," was said almost quietly.

Petunia was about to speak. In the split second in which it took for her mouth to open, a loud cough was heard from somewhere behind the practice manager, its originator presumably thinking this was the only way she was going to stand a chance of interrupting the grandstanding so beloved by the manager.

"Sorry, Ms Makepeace, it was me who opened the letter and placed it in your pigeonhole. I didn't realise it was confidential, I am so sorry."

Amanda's smile deflated like a fallen soufflé, since she herself had placed the letter in the filing room, for the sole purpose of its being opened by the girl she'd deliberately placed there. She'd even gone to the trouble of stamping it, knowing that she could later separate contents from envelope. It couldn't possibly be anyone else who had seen that letter. More alarmingly, she wondered who would want to make the ultimate sacrifice for the new girl in this way – and why. The manager turned round to see Susan looking straight at her, her face immobile and, seemingly, her eyes not even blinking.

The finger was deployed once again but became ever so slightly droopy. "In that case, if it's you, then you are history. Pack your things and go. Go now and get out of my sight." Petunia stared at Susan, her mouth remaining open but shock and surprise precluding speech.

"Very well then, Ms Makepeace."

The manager's face was now neutral as if terminating someone's employment in this way involved the same thoughts as ordering a pizza. None in the office knew her well enough to sense the nuance of fear as she detected completely unknown emotions – someone sacrificing themselves for the greater good.

"I'll have your final cheque sent to you. Please leave forthwith."

Petunia had been unable to foresee any of these events, her mind filling with so many simultaneous thoughts each now queuing with urgency. Even Petunia's active mind could have foreseen neither this outcome nor just how quickly it would be made manifest.

Amanda Makepeace stormed out on her tottering heels. The black patent finish seemed to flash even under the relatively dull overhead lighting of the office. Her tight pencil skirt made her walk seem even more regimented and clipped, as if she were marching to a military band. However, her gait conveyed rather less enthusiasm than when she'd entered. Moreover, her facial expression had been eclipsed by more than slight disappointment, as that of a cultivator of prize marrows on their learning that they'd only managed third prize.

She'd been certain, absolutely certain, that the strategy she'd put in place would guarantee the exit of the suspicious and troublesome new receptionist. She'd never known any of the girls to stick up for another. For sure, they'd mutter a bit, just as they had when Tina departed, but this had never been translated into action of any sort let alone the extreme of a sacrificial act to protect another. It seemed that the new girl had had a positive effect on a great many minds in the surgery including the most threatening one of all, that of Dr Binder. Amanda decided that she was going to have to accelerate her plans. One thing was very clear, she wasn't going to have some untidy girl get in her way when she was so close to achieving success after many months of planning and being among these losers for as long as she had.

The routine of the one departing had a dispassionate and cruel familiarity to it. The empty cardboard boxes that had previously contained the blank prescriptions were a perfect size for the receptionists' meagre effects. Many had taken such a box and placed in it one or two items that should have denoted some degree of comfort in their working environment rather than simply having measured the fleeting nature of their employment.

Susan paused for a minute as she looked round the now hushed office. All eyes returned her gaze as she looked round for one last time. A meagre, wistful smile followed for a second or two before this was swept from her expression by worry. She wasn't sure that she could afford to do what she'd just done. Her dad would be furious. Just one question now pressed with urgency on Petunia's mind. Susan picked up an empty prescription box and started placing in the box one or two personal effects from the shelf in the office that was divided by plywood partitions.

Petunia rushed over to her; she just had to ask as if it was the last question in her life. "Why did you do that? Why did you do that for me?"

Susan looked carefully and intently at her former colleague. "It wasn't for you, Petunia, it was for me and also for all the other girls." Petunia could only stare back, she was so shocked by how quickly events had built that she wasn't sure she could manage further speech just yet. Susan continued, "They say you are the one who can bring her down, give her what she deserves. I thought, at first, when she came, that I hated him more for letting her in," as she pointed to Dr Binder's door.

"Then, I realised he was a victim too. He's still trapped by his own grief and she's the one who kept the surgery running – barely – for some reason entirely to do with her and nothing to do with anyone else. Everyone here is expendable, we knew that the day she arrived. What I hate her for, even more than her selfishness, even more than her cruel ways and even more than her hidden agenda – whatever that may be, is what she's done to me. I used to be like you; bright, friendly; nothing was too much trouble. The patients deserve that; they deserve much better than this excuse for a service. Some say that he'll only have brought on himself what comes to him next week when the CCG inspect and fail him. But I ask myself what'll become of the patients. Even more than all this, however, I can't look myself in the mirror without hating what I see and what I've become. We are supposed, all of us, to be caring people, looking out for the poorly who pitch up here seeking help.

So, you see, this isn't for you, don't flatter yourself: this is purely for me. They say you'll take her; you'll bring her down. I don't know why they say that, but I'm hoping that they are right. I want to know, to at least *believe,* that you are that person. So, don't feel sorry for me, *don't you dare*, I want you to feel much more powerful things than that. You take her, do for her good 'n' proper, and when you've done that perhaps she'll go and this place will, once again, be recruiting good staff, those who will care about what they do and the patients they serve and who'll be encouraged to be the best they can be. When that day arrives, then, you'll know where to find me. Until that day, you do whatever you gotta do, but do that and I'll be waiting for you. Me and lots of others, too."

Little rivulets of tears had begun and, having done so, were now illimitable as they ran down her pale but freckled features: the pale green eyes fading like the moon with only the possibility that a sunny day may come – in the not distant future.

A nod was all that Petunia could manage at this juncture as she finally understood how one person's selfishness and greed could unleash so much suffering. Tears began in her own solid-blue eyes that, like the tears of her colleague, would not stop. Words were inadequate in any event so it was a moot point that her voice had temporarily failed.

She hugged Susan, whose small frame tensed a little at the intrusion, then Petunia offered the simple but impactful words as she pulled back. "I promise."

With this, Susan pressed the little box to her, this representing just about everything she owned in the world. Moving through the main entrance, she continued to walk back up the long road that led to the bus stop – all without looking back. Only one other person saw the tears as they now turned to convulsive sobs that wracked her frame and accompanied each step she took as she struggled, but ultimately failed, to maintain any sort of composure. The wind howled about her, just as it always did in these parts. She clung the little box to her tummy even more, hoping that the cardboard would provide a little warmth and insulation. Had she looked towards the little cottage, she might have seen the net curtains twitch a little as she passed. Mrs Spencer recognised the scene readily enough; sadly it was an all too common occurrence. "Another one gone, Tiddles, and making the long, lonely walk," she said as she looked at the tortoiseshell cat that was winding itself round her legs.

Petunia's cheeks were also stinging with the soaking they'd received from her tears and the hasty sweeps from her palm with which she'd tried to maintain her composure. The room was hushed, once again; a quiet known only to the saddest of funerals had descended throughout the reception. Petunia saw that a new batch of post had arrived, so she departed for the filing room in order to deal with it. The other girls stood silently, by and large, now not daring to speak in case the manager returned precipitously to the office to catch incautious words, as was her wont. All they could risk were stunned looks at one another without even the slightest trace of hope in anyone's eyes.

Annabelle, the youngest, looked down, being unable to meet anyone's gaze. She didn't want anyone to see her looking so sad. She, too, wiped tears away from her face, now swollen and sore, with the back of her hand as she did her best to control her sniffling. It appeared she had to press even more heavily on the reluctant keyboard to persuade it to process prescriptions given the desperate mood that permeated throughout the office, rather like the ever-present dank smell of rotting wood.

That night Petunia busied herself in the office as the other girls hurried out. She saw the manager's black BMW power away, throwing up stones and mud from the surface of the car park as the tyres bit for purchase.

A short time later, as Petunia lingered in the office, a tap appeared on the side door, which she opened carefully peering, into the gathering darkness.

She reached out in order to hold the tall man's hand and led him through to the office conspiratorially. He looked shocked at her appearance; her face that had been watermarked by her tears that had clearly been shed for much of that day. He kissed her as she told him what had happened. He squeezed her hand and sat her on one of her own chairs, the steady brown of his eyes now fired with concern for her and for the others.

Even worse was that he had bad news for her. He took a deep breath, before he began to divulge his new-found information.

"Look, I've run all the reports and it's much worse than we thought. It's even worse that our worst-case scenario. This place is on the brink of disaster. They haven't a prayer of passing the CCG inspection. If they are lucky they'll be given a month, to appeal and so on, but I don't think that will save them. It'll be only a month's grace if they are lucky. This place needs to be completely re-organised and they simply won't agree it. It'll be closed for sure as soon as the niceties are observed. There is absolutely no way it can be saved. I am surprised that it's still open. My contact at the CCG tells me that they were given a warning at their last inspection which was very much seen as the last chance saloon moment. Things have nose-dived since then. I don't know what your *friend* has been doing but saving the surgery is not on her agenda and, it would seem, driving it to destruction seems more likely. My advice is to cut and run now. Leave while you can before you are in too deep and let events take their course."

He'd brought his laptop with him. He placed it on the worktop. He knew that she wouldn't need to see the figures that he'd prepared. She'd be more than happy to accept what he said at face value but he'd brought it just in case.

"Look, I'm not sure I can do that. I offered to help. And now I've promised. These people have been kind to me."

"My love, it's so like you, but that's not enough. Bale out now, before it all goes down.

Offering to help is one thing but professional suicide is another. I just have a bad feeling about it all – there's something else here, something we are not seeing – why is this harridan of a manager here when all there is a failing surgery? Why is she assisting this process rather than trying to prevent it? There's something else in play, a much bigger game and, trust me, you don't want to be in the middle of this. I've sent off your photos and video to an expert. He'll come back to me soon. We may know more then but it's not going to change the depths to which this surgery has sunk."

"But they have also sacrificed themselves for me. They have lost their jobs because of me."

"I know, my love, and it was so kind of that girl to do that for you." He then corrected his own words, "to do that for the greater good."

"And then there's the letter."

"I know, my darling, but just think, please. Anyone could have sent that letter. You have no idea who sent it, nor what their part is in all this. You can't save a dying surgery, you'll get hurt and this is not what we do. We have other projects, others to save and there'll be another day for us."

"Not if we let them down, when we can't look them or each other in the eye."

"I know what's colouring your view now apart from that letter. That poor girl who left today: she made her own decision. You don't owe her anything. You don't owe *them* anything." Even as he said the words he knew that Petunia would take the very opposite tack.

"Always, always, I do! I just can't let them burn. Burn here in this purgatory. We promised, all those months ago, that we would help wherever and whenever. We can't just pull out now. That is not what we do. Is it?"

She'd left the question open, he was welcome to supply his own views and for a moment his mouth moved just a little and only then did he begin to speak.

"I just have a feeling, a bad feeling, that we will go down with this ship. Are you prepared for that?"

"Yes, I think I am. Then, if we go down, we go down. Are you with me?"

He looked at her, his words having failed. How could he not be with her? How could he ever be without her? He smiled and kissed her again. For sure it had never been a joint promise, but he knew that sometimes the unspoken promises were the strongest that could exist between two people. He knew, in any event, that it was one that bound them both. She'd started it; she began the work months before he made the discovery. But having learned of what she was about and what she planned, how could he not have gone along with those plans – and with her. Moreover, he knew, he'd always known, that this is what made her so special, simply unique in a selfish and greedy world. She shone amongst those who'd do dark deeds. Ultimately, he knew that this is what had forged her, what drove her and he couldn't change that any more than he could change those beautiful eyes that glowed like pale sapphires seemingly alight on a moonlit night.

"I just knew you were going to say that," he smiled and kissed her forehead.

"Well then, in that case you also knew that you'd be wasting your breath."

"I just had to mention it, you know how I like to look out for you and your interests."

"Always, always, my love and don't think that I'm not grateful. And I've told you, they are *our* interests," she kissed him lightly and continued. "Now, what are we going to do?"

He had no time to respond, for Emma Sparkle came rushing in. They both turned round with a start as she rushed in, still dragging her cleaner's trolley.

"She's coming. Hide!"

"Ms Makepeace is here? She's come back?" Petunia looked quickly back at him, her face now etched with alarm.

The cleaner had no time to answer questions. She was already thinking of a way of protecting the two young people who had been stunned by the unexpected events and also by her precipitous entry. All she could do was nod. Without further ado the cleaner opened the stationery cupboard and pushed the big man inside in one smooth, deft move as if she were simply throwing rubbish in a skip. He clattered to the back of the cupboard but mercifully managed to suppress a yell as his knee caught a metallic object.

At that moment Amanda Makepeace arrived. She strode in and, without looking at the people she expected to see, she looked round the room.

"It's late. I see you are still here, Miss Mumple? And who were you talking to?"

"I was talking to Emma, Ms Makepeace." Petunia did her best to look nonplussed and surprised as to how the manager could not know who she had been talking to.

"Emma?"

"Yes, Ms Makepeace, Emma Sparkle, the senior cleaner."
Petunia now nodded towards the cleaner as if underlining
what surely must be obvious. The manager's embarrassment
at not knowing the name of the cleaner, in fact none of the
three cleaners' names, probably saved Petunia from further
scrutiny. That fact alone was enough to distract the manager
from her stern inquisition and also the quick thinking of Mrs
Sparkle.

"Oh, oh yes, of course." She muttered quickly, having to
hide, equally quickly, the fact that she had no idea who the
cleaner was, let alone her name.

"Why are you here so late, then?"

Petunia hesitated, but the cleaner was already fielding the
question. "She's forgotten her bus ticket, Ms Makepeace. Here
you are, girlie, you young uns would forget your heads if they
weren't screwed on, you would." Emma then produced a bus
ticket which she held up prominently and handed it over to the
young receptionist who seamlessly took it as she did her best
to suppress any hint of surprise.

The manager could have sworn that she'd heard voices, and
unrecognised ones, from the office as she'd crept back. She
scanned the room urgently, once more, but by now the
moment had passed and her chance of discovery was
irrevocably damaged. She looked round at the printers and the
computer screens. All of these had been switched off and not
one tell-tale light appeared.

"Were you not talking to a man?" she glared at the
receptionist.

"A man? No, Ms Makepeace as you can see it's just the
two of us," replied Emma in her straightforward tone.

"I was just showing Miss Mumple here out through the
front door now that she has her bus ticket." Petunia moved
obligingly towards the door. It was then that she saw the
laptop that had been left on the table. Its gleaming, slim case
was readily visible. Emma followed the young woman's line
of sight. She had never used a laptop. She had no idea how to

use a computer let alone such a slim, powerful and sophisticated device. She was sufficiently aware, however, to detect that the laptop that had been left in plain view by the tall man, now doing his best to breathe quietly in the cupboard, was not of the surgery. Much more than this, she detected that it was a high-end item and not the sort of kit that even the most technologically motivated receptionist would either need or even be able to afford.

Mercifully, Emma had tracked the flicker of the gaze from the manager still scanning round the room. The manager very rarely looked at people anyway so was not in a position to detect the transient alarm on each woman's face. Emma knew, however, that her sharp and unfeeling gaze would soon alight on the table that held the object that was a stranger to the surgery and to a receptionist.

From her cleaner's trolley she somehow managed to scoop up a sheaf of bright yellow refuse sacks and placed them on the table in order to cover the laptop.

"Right then young Miss, as I said I have work to do round here and I can't be spending my time looking for your lost bus tickets now can I? Dr Binder and Ms Makepeace here will have my guts for garters. Let's be avin' you, then, girlie." She smacked her hands together in a business-like fashion.

Emma moved to the half-glazed pair of wooden doors with the wood stain that didn't quite match the panelling that had long since become dark and shiny with the patina of age and hundreds of hands being employed to push against it. Petunia grabbed the bus ticket and walked towards the open door that Emma had held open for her.

"Goodnight, Mrs Sparkle, Ms Makepeace," she offered cordially.

The manager's depth of thought precluded any further speech. Emma saw the receptionist through the door and moved to reach up for the locking latch, whispering as she did so, "You owe me a bus ticket, girlie."

The young receptionist managed a conspiratorial smile and also mouthed a 'thank you' as she made her exit from the building. Emma closed the door with a well-practised flick of her wrist in the third of her deft moves that evening.

Turning now to the tall, unusually immobile practice manager who remained now as might a detective on being called to the scene of a crime only to discover that some vital clue lay before her but was as yet unseen.

"Do you need me, Ms Makepeace or shall I get on?"

Rather than grace the poor woman with any words, Amanda offered only her back by way of reply as she turned and left the room. Conversing with cleaners was well below her station. The only heed the manager paid to the eager and hard-working woman was to decide that Emma's name would be added to the long list of those about to lose their jobs. Five minutes later Amanda went through the rear door for the final time that evening.

Only then did Emma deem it safe to open the cupboard door. The tall man who'd sought sanctuary there almost fell out as his crouched frame was finally given some release. He rubbed his knee as he exited from the uncomfortable refuge.

"Good job it's only a sore knee, laddo. If that manager 'ad found ya, I don't know what she would'a done? I'm guessing you'll want to be on yer way with girlie over yonder. You nearly got us all in trouble, I'll wager," she concluded as she nodded to the door through which Petunia had vacated the building some minutes before. "And, I'm assumin' that you two are still both workin' to help Dr Binder?"

"We hope so, Mrs Sparkle," he replied, his deep brown eyes shining for a moment before they were subsumed by the bright smile that seemed to have the same resonance as that of the young receptionist.

"I'm guessin', too, that this is yours," Emma said, as she uncovered the wafer-thin laptop from under the stack of polythene bags and handed it to him stroking a rough palm over its refined, smooth and unruffled surface.

He took it gratefully. "Ah yes, that was such quick thinking, many thanks."

"I just hope you two young uns can bring about some change here, For sure, it can't get any worse."

"I hope so too, Mrs Sparkle. Thank you for helping us."

"Nowt else for it, for sure. This whole place will go to the dogs if we don't do summat."

She let the handsome man out through the double doors and went about her cleaning routine with something of curiosity, delight and satisfaction now orbiting her consciousness in equal parts.

CHAPTER VIII

Inspection

Emma was wrong, for it was about to get much worse. Monday was upon them in no time and only Amanda Makepeace greeted it with something of unabridged delight. Without doubt, she did her best to hide her ebullient mood from any observer but given the depths of hatred with which she'd run the surgery for the past months, very few could fail to notice the change in her. She waited eagerly and restlessly in the office so she could detect the first signs of the arrival of the representatives of the CCG and the CCA. Although nobody knew it, she'd approached the CCG to see if the planned meeting could be brought forward. Recent events involving their new receptionist had unsettled her and she guessed that her best strategy now was to strike and strike fast, long before the interloper could even begin to guess what game was really in play here.

She laughed to herself when she thought about it having very little to do with the surgery. The whole place and, especially, the people who worked within its dingy confines were pawns in a much greater game and it would be a miracle if any of them were able to stop her now. The other point that caused her even greater merriment was the fact that she was about to destroy the whole shooting match simply by raising one little finger.

As soon as she heard the cars drawing up, Amanda flew down the stairs from her first floor office with a spring in her step. She had waited patiently for the end-game to build. She had planned for such a thing and here it was about to be set in motion. The final act was upon them.

Amanda greeted the inspectors, two from the CCG and two from the CCA. Just as they arrived, Dr Binder also appeared at the door but with very different emotions: as a man approaching the gallows might have written on his perpetually sad expression.

The team of four were led through reception by the manager who fussed about their guests like a bride at her own wedding. Some of the receptionists had made an effort, looking as if they'd pressed their burgundy blouses. The cleaners, too, had made herculean efforts to raise a shine on the tired and aged surfaces, but notwithstanding such labours the whole place was unable to shrug off its neglected image. It was almost as if a temporary shine had been applied to a car that barely disguised the deep and extensive rust that permeated throughout.

For once the repeat prescription trays, as well as the filing trays, had been emptied. No amount of token organising from such a small and demoralised band could conceal either the patients who still queued restlessly, or the overall feeling of unrestrained chaos with their haphazard flow through the poorly-managed building. Moreover, the ever-present antiquated and overwhelmed computer system made little pretence at coping with a modern primary care setting. Amanda thought to herself that all of them, staff, doctors and patients were about to be put out of their misery and the CCG and CCA were about to do her work for her. In an even more elegant and precise analysis it occurred to her that it was their duty to do just that. She smiled wickedly to herself and no longer worried whether anyone noticed: she would soon be out of this dreary place.

As the inspectors moved through the surgery they, too, saw the hopelessness written on the girls' faces – the saturated clinics and the over-dependence on locums who could never be expected to remain for long enough to get to know the patients in sufficient detail to provide them with even a semblance of the service they had a right to expect.

Much more than this, there had clearly been no attempt to provide what would be considered the bare minimum; the necessities required of any modern surgery, such as a resuscitation trolley, an oxygen cylinder and basic drugs such as adrenaline for use in the unlikely but catastrophic event of a collapsed patient. On being questioned, the receptionists admitted that they had never heard of such things and even the practice nurse seemed very vague on the need for and use of such equipment. The inspectors' eyes stared wide with incredulity as they struggled to find one positive attribute on a long list of tick boxes that were steadily damning the surgery as they progressed down. One inspector wrote on his confidential notes that the surgery had singlehandedly set general practice back at least fifty years.

Never acknowledged, let alone admitted, was the fact that locums were expensive and inefficient prescribers. They had no grounding to the surgery nor did they have any particular loyalty. Most of them would be working elsewhere the following day. To this end they often prescribed too many and unnecessary antibiotics and a great many other items that led to the surgery exceeding its drug budget, and also caused it to be marked as an outlier when judged against modern protocols. This did not sit easily with the modern cash-constrained NHS. Likewise, a locum might offer temporary solutions so that the patient would have to come back or make unnecessary referrals that the patient didn't need when a review in a week or two would often suffice.

All this served as a warm-up to the main event, which was more than hinted at by the thick binders containing information that they'd brought with them. The dismal performance as revealed by their initial inspection could be fixed and therefore excused. People could be trained up or new, more capable staff could be employed. The reports they carried were far more damaging and more than hinted at longstanding underperformance, which was both unsafe and, although never admitted publically, expensive. These printouts detailed the surgery performance over a wide variety of key indicators. These, together with the reports furnished by the surgery computer, would form the biggest affirmation that the surgery had reached a dark apogee. One of the inspectors confided quietly to a colleague that they'd been responsible for failing other surgeries that had in place much better procedures and facilities.

The team of four were led up the stairs and into the meeting room. One of the receptionists had been detailed to offer hot drinks as an alternative to the cold drinks that had been placed on the table. The four sat at the back of the dark table feeling very uncomfortable. How much easier their role was when visiting excellent, well-performing surgeries or even those that were simply average, but safe. This practice was in neither of those categories.

It was incontrovertible that every GP surgery in the land was now subject to intense and far reaching scrutiny. Although politicians of all parties had tried to disown this fact, each GP was requested, and required, to slash costs as never before, whilst raising their game as regards the hours they opened and the facilities and range of services they provided. The public face of this dichotomy was hidden behind the façade of the mantra that was trotted out by all politicians whenever they were interviewed. They would all speak stridently of the unlimited resources not only available to each and every patient but also free at the point of delivery. All parties recognised the political suicide that would accompany even admitting that this was no longer the case and indeed had not been during several changes of government. Nor could they ever admit to the number of private providers who'd been supplying services to the NHS and its patients for the past ten years or more.

The simple, but well hidden, fact was that GPs were now measured simply by how much they cost the public purse.

Every GP had almost engraved on their eyelids an ever-lengthening list of which activities generated which costs. Thus the cost burden that a casualty attendance, a hip operation, a gastroscopy or a month's supply of anti-ulcer or blood pressure treatment would place upon the public finances had been calculated with unswerving and far-reaching precision for every GP in the land. Such considerations were masked under the heading of "GP costs".

The tacit expectation was that in the modern NHS the GP's main role was to drive costs down. To this end a sophisticated array of information was now held about each GP and surgery in England. What were the true costs of their prescribing, how many patients took themselves off to casualty, how many referrals were made to hospital, how much district nurses cost and, one of the most difficult to encompass, the NEL or non-elective admissions. These, in particular, represented those patients who had the temerity to turn up at their local Casualty department and were then promptly admitted. This was often for legitimate reasons but unfortunately costs of such an activity were very high, heading even higher and were extremely difficult for every general practice, even the most efficiently run, to keep under control. This, then, would be the rock that would break the back of the tiny ship that represented the West Pennine surgery. Not only were such efficiencies not in place, but it lacked even the basic standards and would not even approach, let alone surpass, the minimum requirements for a modern surgery.

It was widely believed that GPs had control of such spending and widespread autonomy over such services via the CCG but the reality was that they had the responsibility but not necessarily the control over any of it. They were simply expected to conform to the basic minimum of service provision whilst controlling their spending. These facts were now inevitably about to bring down Dr Binder on several levels.

The visitors sat and muttered, shook their heads, raked their fingers through their hair, and incessantly recorded damning scores on their clipboards. They looked, or at least went through the motions of looking, for positives, but the tale of woe seemed to become more all-pervading and unavoidable the more they looked. Mostly, they looked sad, for none of the inspectors liked to fail a practice. Moreover, the more they looked the more they could see that, in this case, it was so clear cut as to allow them to arrive at their conclusions as soon as they had reached the end of the files they'd been leafing through.

Mrs Freemont, head of the surgery inspectorate at the CCA was unable to meet the GP's eye. Bad news was so much harder to give than good and perhaps it was easier not to look at the man who seemed as sorrowful today as he had been the last time they'd met, now some three years ago.

She decided that a dispassionate, detached air would get her through. Her sympathies for the wretched man had no place here: not if she was to do her job properly. She knew something of the trials he had been through and also acknowledged the loyalty of his patients. Indeed, patient surveys had revealed overall satisfaction with the GPs and the services at the surgery. This was the only bright spot against a litany of failings. Ultimately, she was expected to do her job and her personal sadness at her task had no place here as she reminded herself that they'd failed much better establishments.

Mrs Freemont positioned her glasses well up the slope of her nose so that she did not have to look over the top of them at the unhappy GP. Dr Rapace was delighted that he'd not been required to attend the meeting and remained downstairs running the surgery alongside two locums. Between patients, he continued to press the builders ever harder to finish his new surgery on time and within budget.

Mrs Freemont coughed before she began and found herself gulping on a glass of water. "I'm sorry but these figures are atrocious, some of the worst we've come across and so much worse than those of your peers, not just in West Pennine, but also across the region as a whole. Perhaps even more telling is that they have deteriorated even further since your last inspection. As I am sure you remember from our last visit, we usually like to take figures away, peruse them at our leisure in some detail and then report back in a week or so. However, with these figures," she raised a piece of paper distastefully and let it fall, "there is a disaster wherever we look. I am so sorry, Dr Binder, but there is no alternative to our giving you four weeks' notice of closure. We propose to declare your surgery non-viable exactly twenty-eight days from now.

"As you know, you do have the right of appeal. This, however, carries two conditions. The first is that you provide us with new evidence for us to consider, or extenuating circumstances to be brought to our attention. I see that you exercised this option at our last visit and we agreed, somewhat reluctantly, it has to be said, to an extension. It will be very unlikely that you will be allowed to use such criteria again. The second condition, as I must remind you, is that these proceedings remain confidential and any information that is leaked will immediately render our offer null and void. In such circumstances we will close you down with no further notice. Subsequently the entire patient list of over eight thousand souls will be notified and dispersed across any other bidders who come forward. Failing this, in the advent of no willing alternative providers of GP services, then the existing GP providers in and around this locality will be required to take them."

Dr Binder looked crestfallen, now displaying misery rather than the usual ennui that hung about him like a saddle on an exhausted horse that was about to collapse.

"Are you clear about what I am saying to you?" emphasised Mrs Freemont, as only in that moment did she attempt to look at him.

Amanda Makepeace sat in silence next to her boss. She was making a valiant attempt to prevent the delight from appearing in force on her expression. She coughed and she looked down at the reports but even a glance at her self-satisfied features would reveal that she knew her time, everything that she had worked for, was about to come to pass. She was proud of herself and her unstinting efforts. It was true that if she'd taken a crane and a wrecking ball, then she could not have done a more complete job of destroying the surgery. Of much greater importance was that she'd brought it down just at the right time. Any earlier and others might detect what she'd helped to hide and any later would delay the plans of her real employers. She smiled even more when she heard the chief inspector mention the period of grace and the option of an appeal. Although she'd assumed that they would offer such a thing, Amanda had no time for such delay as there was a much more significant and far-reaching game in play. Her plan was like a fine wine that had received utmost care and attention from the vintner and was now ready to provide a career-making return. She was about to taste that wine and enjoy it to the full.

Dr Binder looked down. He realised in that moment that his grief had held him hostage for five years. More importantly, he realised that his wife, Jenny, would not want this for him. This would hurt so much, almost as if she had died afresh or the loving memory that he held of her was also now about to be forfeit. She would have insisted that he stand; that he be the GP that she'd recognised and fallen in love with; one who'd supported and nourished his practice, his patients and his staff. He should not simply allow them to drift on to disaster. He'd presided over rack and ruin and just at the moment where the enormity of the catastrophe that faced him became clear, he realised that it was already too late to change. He'd let Jenny down and their precious little boy, as well as himself. Moreover, he had failed all those who had remained loyal, those who looked to him to care for them, everyone who'd depended on him to show courage and be the GP they'd always remembered.

He'd basically been asleep for the last five years and now, as he awoke from the dream he could only embrace the nightmare that was in fact his life. Paradoxically, by drifting through the days and by not confronting the issues that lay around him, he'd allowed himself to be lulled into a life that was a lot more comforting. No, he had to accept that it was rather more than this. He'd been numbed to just about everything and he'd been sleep-walking to the vista that now lay before him. So many had pinned their hopes on him and he'd been responsible for failing them all.

He stared into the distance. Mrs Freemont was still speaking to him. Her voice was raised; she'd clearly had to repeat herself.

"So, Dr Binder I must ask you once again, are you *clear* about what I am saying?"

He nodded rather hurriedly as he struggled to get back into the proceedings.

"And, Doctor, are you clear what avenues remain open to you?"

He nodded again, now frightened to speak.

"Are you aware of your right of appeal and the conditions that have been applied to this?"

"I am, Mrs Freemont, thank you," he whispered as he managed speech at last.

"Then, it looks as though this meeting is closed. You have my secretary's number should you need to contact me."

The four inspectors rose to go; surely he must also stand. Amanda, however, had already shot to her feet being the hostess that she should be. He, too, could at least be polite. He managed a few words hoping that they would at least convey a little politeness but they appeared more of a grunt rather than the more well-mannered tones he usually offered, as the disaster unfolding around him had remorselessly consumed him.

He knew in that moment that he was about to lose everything

Amanda returned, having shown them to the exit.

"Whoosh, they were much more harsh than I'd anticipated," she lied. They'd performed exactly as she expected. Moreover, just to make sure, she'd placed a call a few days before to the head of the CCG as well as the CCA posing as a concerned patient asking them if they were going to do their duty in performing their forthcoming inspection. Amanda had been assured in her guise of the bogus caller that proper procedures would be followed without fear or favour.

Her attention snapped back to the room though she had trouble muting her devious and self-satisfied smile which lingered as she spoke. "Well, at least we have a month," she lied again, knowing that her plans would no longer allow him even a month. "I'm sure in this time we can put a case together as to why you should be allowed to continue on the Principal list and provider of GMS."

She now stared almost coyly at him. "Only, I was wondering if you'd had a chance to speak with Dr Rapace at all," her voice now at its most entreating but also at its most false.

"It's just that I heard he's thinking of a change." The delicate pauses she'd crafted deliberately into her words were designed to show caring and concern but the exact opposite emotions now ran within her. Dark eyes glistened hungrily as they looked at him.

"A change? What sort of change."

Her seed having been sown, she now placed false modesty on her words.

"I'm not too sure." She shrugged her shoulders disingenuously, knowing precisely what sort of change Dr Rapace was intending – one that had absolutely no place for the senior partner, his friend.

"Well, perhaps the two of you need to talk? In any event, we have a month."

Amanda left the senior partner to his own thoughts. He sat and placed his head in his hands, running through the events of the day over and over again. This is precisely what his manager had intended. She knew that his own thoughts would ultimately sow the seeds of his own destruction.

Dr Binder knew only that he needed time. Time to do so many things that he should have done years ago. Time to think; to reflect, to create a future strategy that would ensure the survival of his surgery and, most of all, time for a complete re-invention of himself. Yes, this is what Jenny would say to him if she were still here. This is what he had to do.

It was fortuitous that he'd got a month in to bring about some of the desperately needed changes – time that he now knew was essential. He would sit down with his practice manager over the next few days and they could plot a strategy to rejuvenate the surgery and get it back on its feet again. He reckoned that, although the timing was a bit tight, twenty-eight days would be enough to get some serious proposals together, with help from Amanda.

In point of fact, the confidentiality that Mrs Freemont had insisted on lasted barely an hour. As soon as Amanda Makepeace got back to her desk, after closing the door carefully, she picked up her phone. The long index finger with the talon-like acrylic nail extended in a move that would make sure of his departure and guarantee, at the same time, that her own plans were firmly in the ascendant. And this was all it took; the lifting of one purposeful finger. She dialled the number that she now knew off by heart.

The phone rang on the desk of her contact at the *Horwich Chronicle*. It was answered immediately for he'd been anticipating her call. He listened intently but nevertheless could not prevent himself from hopping animatedly around his desk as the explosive and damaging revelations from the private and confidential meeting were released to him.

The reporter's delight knew no bounds.

"Another wonderful story, Ms Makepeace, I can't thank you enough. It looks like you've made my career. Just when I thought it was all over for me, here you are with another exclusive. Should get my promotion that's been in the offing. Now, just what do you need from me in return?"

She smiled distastefully as she heard his words. Men were so easy to manipulate and the irony was that they were always so grateful for having been so influenced. "Nothing, absolutely nothing, for now. Just print what I've told you on the front page in the biggest letters your paper can manage, as soon as you can. I'll phone you if and when I need a favour. Actually, come to think of it, I wonder if you could check someone out for me? There's a receptionist who's been making trouble and this is why I've brought forward my plans. My boss isn't quite ready to make his move but she is trouble, I know it. She's just a bit too smart. Although she looks like a shaggy dog, what's going on in that untidy head of hers has surprised and unsettled me."

"Have you any details for her?"

"I'll fax you what I do have and I also have a picture of her, it's a bit small and not very distinct. She looks like that girl on 'The Magic Roundabout'." The reporter had never seen the Magic Roundabout but he found himself nodding in agreement. His source had singlehandedly done so much to help him in re-launching his career, he'd have agreed with her if she told him about the green cheese that the moon was made of, or that he was in league with someone of whom the devil himself would be very proud. In fact he'd be in accord with anything and anyone that would ensure the smooth flow of confidential and restricted information for him to cause his journalistic career to rise a few more notches.

"Anyway, see what you make of her? I've checked with the agency that sent her, and spoken to the people who supplied her with references. It's all drawn a blank and she seems squeaky clean but I just have this feeling about her."

"So, fax me her picture and I can start with that."

"It's not a good one. I'll fax what I have and you can do some digging for me – you owe me big time after my singlehandedly resurrecting your career for you."

"I know who my friends are, don't you worry, and I'll find out who she is."

The reception staff, as usual, were kept in the dark and given very little news. Certainly, none of their number were aware that the surgery, their place of work, had a limited viability stretching before it, that could now be measured in days. Eventually after some careful listening added to conjecture and gossip they came to the conclusion that the surgery had been granted a reprieve during which time it was to demonstrate its on-going fitness to practise medicine and General Medical Services.

Ultimately, all they could do was continue to do their jobs as far as they were allowed to whilst remaining, at all times, under the whip hand of their manager, who would surely punish like a galley slave anyone who failed to follow her orders or who even attempted to seek a little sunshine on their face.

That night the tall man waited for Petunia in the little car that was parked in the shadows as she came through the double and half-glazed front doors. She entered the car and kissed him. She knew, however, by the anxious look and pauses in his sentences that there was something he had to tell her.

She waited patiently. He hesitated and cleared his throat before speaking.

"It seems your suspicions were well founded. I've made some enquiries as to who is at work on the moorland. They have analysed the photos you took and the video footage. I am afraid it confirms your worst fears." He handed her a file with information about the company that had been at work on the moors at night. "Ms Makepeace is their employee. This is why she is here and why she has deliberately run the surgery into the ground. They'd never be able to advance their plans with a surgery here, it would be the kiss of death. There is a much bigger game in play and I can only advise you..."

His voice trailed away, she began to nod, knowing, only too well, what he'd been about to say.

"I know what you are telling me and I know that we have entered some treacherous waters. I just know that I have to keep going. I can't just desert all these people, the ones that I came here to help."

"I know, my love. It's just that there is a lot of money, huge corporate funds, if I am not mistaken, riding on this," he paused again, wanting his words to sink in but in truth he knew she'd have already worked out for herself the risks that they were running.

She nodded, acknowledging as always the care and attention he showed her at all times, even when they disagreed.

"I'm guessing that it will come down to money and lots of it. I wouldn't be surprised if you end up having to commit every penny you have. And even then it'll still be a gamble and remember just who you will be going up against." He tapped the file on her knee with his index finger. "They are probably funded by some really big firms even private equity like the pension funds who have very deep pockets, not to mention some of the biggest firms on the London Stock Exchange. Even worse, if she catches wind of who you are then it could make things very difficult. They haven't just chanced upon this place and this opportunity. Just how long do you think they've been out there? They aren't going to just walk away after the money they must have put in so far. This is like a poker game where you have to commit vast sums just to see their hand with no guarantee that you'll win. It will take every penny you've got. You could be ruined. You'd be mad to go forward with this."

Petunia swallowed hard; she knew that he wasn't exaggerating. In truth it was only what she'd been telling herself. Moreover, she wasn't surprised to learn what was really behind this cruel and entirely bogus façade. People's lives, the patients and the staff were simply an unwanted aside and had no bearing in the real game that was in play. This is why the manager had adopted the strategy she had. The last thing she wanted was a viable thriving surgery. It must irk her considerably to see that Dr Binder remained popular despite her best efforts to bring the place down.

"They are sending up a drone tomorrow if it's not too windy. That will allow them to survey the whole site, if possible. This should give us more information as to the extent of the operation over there and some idea of the funds that must be underpinning it. However, I don't think it will alter the economics of the deal or the warnings that it contains. It certainly won't alter who you are up against."

She managed a weak smile but the trembling of her fringe said much more: he knew of no previous occasion when she'd shown so much fear.

She smiled, now with more conviction as she brightened. "Look, I've told you before, it's every penny *we've* got and who *we* are up against." She looked steadily at him, her confidence flooding back as he knew that he was unable to respond in that moment: when she looked at him this way his own voice would surely tremble too much. He could already feel his knees shaking just a little.

"Well then, I reckon we go on and that's exactly what we're going to do: after all, I promised," continued Petunia.

"You and your promises. I just knew that you'd say that." He bent just a little to kiss her, the quiet whisper now in her ear. "Just so you know. I'll still love you when you're poor."

"You'd better, besides, as I said, it's when we're poor!"

"Whatever you say, my darling. Loving you could never have a value placed upon it."

"You've not been reading those romantic birthday cards again have you?"

"Mm, I can feel a new career coming on when we are penniless."

"I'm not sure that writing romantic verses for cards is that lucrative."

"Well, I suppose I'll just have to go back to my old job, then."

"Always, always a good idea, that. I might go back to mine, too."

Chapter IX

Non-Viable

Dr Binder saw the front page of the *Horwich Chronicle* the following morning. It was plain that the newspaper had somehow gained access to confidential information; the chosen headline was unmissable to all who might even glance at the paper. 'Non-Viable!' it rang out in the largest font that would fit the tabloid.

Below the brutal headline came an equally brutal article penned by their newly-promoted senior reporter; a detailed exposition of the failures and shortcomings of the once-venerated surgery. Dr Binder stared at the front page. He knew in that moment that it was all over for him. The CCG would take a very dim view of their requirements being made public in this way. They would punish him severely for such a transgression. His time had run out and only closure, with a likely dispersal of all their patients, lay ahead. He knew that all the staff would be devastated by the events that would surely come into being over the next few days and they would all be as surprised and shocked as he was. He could not think where such a leak might have come from. In any event it represented the worst of news for them all. Little did he realise that others had been hatching very different plans.

Dr Rapace was the first to bang on his door. This was his moment, the moment he'd been working towards for the past two years. Now it was upon him and he was ready to deliver the coup-de-grace; to put his partner out of his misery. He could only conclude that this is what someone should have done months ago, like putting down an old, blind dog that was surely of no use to anyone.

"Look, sorry about this Neil, and I hope you won't despise me too much for saying this, but it's really time for me to consider my own future. I really need a place of my own, as the teenager says to his mum and dad." The lips moved to frame the laugh, but the dark eyes betrayed no sense of pleasantness. "I've bought the old cinema in the centre of town and workers are renovating it as we speak. It should be ready very soon."

"But, Fergus, just what will you do for patients?"

Only the pause alluded to his naivety.

"Well, old chap, of course, I'll take all of mine and, not to beat about the bush, I've put in a bid to the CCA to take over yours as well. Frightfully sorry about this, old chap."

"Oh I see," he replied, the short words not really doing justice to the avalanche of thoughts that now dawned on him like the sun coming up over a barren and desolate valley.

"So what happens to me?" he asked superfluously. Dr Binder now looked very old, very tired and crestfallen.

"Sorry about this, but, you know, some say that you died, too, in that car five years ago. You've only got yourself to blame." He tried to put long pauses between his words but ultimately, his haste at getting the words out and moving on proved too strong a temptation. "Look, Neil, we really have to consider the patients, don't you think, eh?" he lied almost convincingly.

Dr Rapace had really no more words to say: it was over. It'd been over a long time before. Only the senior partner had not recognised that sometimes the dead still stood: for surely, no one had told them to lie down. That juncture was now to hand. It was time for him to take up a more suitable situation.

Amanda Makepeace knew that Dr Rapace was delivering his bombshell to his former friend and former partner. She knew this would be the last brick coming away that would cause the whole wall to topple.

Her first phone call, while she contemplated the cosy feeling and the more literal dividend of success, was to her contact at the *Horwich Chronicle*.

"Nice work! You really got the knife out. This will bring him down for sure. As soon as the CCA see that front page and I am told some wicked, wicked person has already sent it anonymously in the post to them."

"It's what I do best, darlin'. I really stuck it to them. They thought I was finished, good for nowt. Well, I'll show them when I use this promotion to get an even better job. They won't be laughing at me then."

She knew how the conversation would go when he lapsed into his bitter routines. She interrupted quickly, "How did you get on with the photos of our receptionist, soon to be ex-receptionist? Oh, and congratulations on your promotion. I see you are now senior reporter. And, by the way, please don't call me darling."

"Sorry, Ms Makepeace. Thank you for the feedback. Always like to know when my work is appreciated and I love getting' the knife out and stickin' it in some grammar school boy who thinks he's better than anyone else. That photo is no good, all I can see of her is that fringe. Could be the Dulux dog for all I know," he opined. "I've also phoned all of the referees, they all trot the same words out. The other strange thing is that medical staffing agency were offered this girl by another medical staffing agency and, guess what, I can't seem to find a trace of them?

It just don't add up. What time does she finish tomorrow night? I'm gonna meet up with Miss Dulux and see what's under that fringe. I'll find out who she is. I never like to let these cocky bastards get the better of me. I always do for 'em, sooner or later. Like my predecessor, I told her she was out of her depth and couldn't cut it just bein' a woman. Needs a man to really stick the knife in. She ran out in tears, I reckon she won't be back." Just then the reporter paused as he realised who he was taking to. "Beggin' your pardon like, you bein' the exception n'all."

He then went on, feeling that he'd said too much and realising that each word was making things worse. Finally, he concluded, "She won't escape me. I've been doin' this job too long to let some kid beat me. The bitch won't beat me, that's a promise."

"Well, perhaps concentrate on this girl and let me know if you have any more information," she said before putting the phone down quickly on the insufferable misogynist, who in truth seemed to hate just about everyone, she concluded with a shrug of her shoulders.

The second phone call was of far greater significance. It was so important that it could have caused her whole strategy to come undone.

She dabbed excitedly at her smartphone as she saw the name of her boss and lover appear.

"Felix, so nice to hear from you, my love. Just wrapping things up here. I am really hoping we can meet up in the next day or two. Let me know if your wife is working away, won't you? It looks as though this surgery is finished, it will literally be an empty shell within a couple of weeks. There's no way they can recover from this. Backstabbing Fergus Rapace is downstairs as we speak just delivering the last rites. I reckon we'll be all set by the end of the month."

"Ah, yes, Mandy, well done! Nobody could have pulled this off like you. This is why you are my most capable, most trusted..." only the pause hid what he really thought of her, but he carried on quickly, "you've done so well. There's a large bonus waiting here for you as soon as we have the agreement in place. Actually, that is why I am phoning. There's been a delay in the cash drawdown. Our finance won't be in place for a week or two. This makes us vulnerable if someone should discover what we are up to and what we plan to do with that expanse of worthless moorland. Is there any way you can delay things there?"

"Oh Felix, I brought things forward because of a sneaky feeling I have about one of the receptionists. I am sure she is up to no good and I can't help but think she is out of place here. I just wonder if she's on to us and if she's guessed that we have other fish to fry. I am sure she won't have the resources to derail us but I just have a bad feeling about her. Look, just get the funds in place as soon as you can and I will try to delay things here. Hopefully it's too late anyway even if someone does guess what's going on."

"Mandy, I know I can count on you. Yes, Sheila will be away the weekend after next, so if you want to meet up at the usual place, that's fine with me."

"Okay, I'll be in touch before then. I'll get a room booked."

The manager was worried. Something about the new girl had unsettled her and she was rarely wrong about such things. Indeed, her presence had forced her hand into moving more quickly than she would have liked. If funds were not available and soon, then disaster could befall them, especially if their secrets were to be uncovered. In many ways this was the crucial time when success was nearly theirs and yet could be snatched away from them without warning.

It was at such times, however, when things seemed to be moving away from her that Amanda was at her most brilliant and, by the time her agile mind had booked a room so that she could meet up with her lover, she had already compassed a solution. Like all the best solutions the idea that came to her was simple, easy to implement and would be far-reaching in its effect. In point of fact, putting such a strategy in place would not only lead to assured success for her, but would also destroy everyone around her, including anyone who so much as tried to move against her.

Quickly she addressed her laptop and within minutes she had drawn up and printed the forms she would need to cement her victory.

With this she left her office and became the second person to knock on Dr Binder's door that afternoon.

She tapped confidently, almost proprietorially on Dr Binder's door. At his greatest moment of weakness, courtesy of his less than loyal partner, it was now time for her to strike and she knew that this was the moment upon which her entire strategy would turn. She tossed her head back with an easy confidence but then did her best to generate a more guileless aura. She knew that he'd always done precisely what she'd asked of him; this was why he was now in such a mess. Hopefully, he would fail to see through any of her latest plans just as he'd failed to see the real events for the past twelve months.

She began quietly, almost demurely; ways of behaviour which were themselves strange visitors to her persona. "Sorry about this Dr Binder, Dr Rapace has made me an offer I can't refuse. I'm sorry to leave like this but I think we can all see that the writing's on the wall." He looked as a captain might who'd not only lost his rudder but now his main mast too, with only a harsh and rocky lee shore waiting for him off his port bow as his tiny, vulnerable ship drifted ever nearer. Just when he knew it was all over, that he had absolutely nothing left, she made her suggestion. He nodded, mumbled something about at least allowing some to save themselves, and in that moment she knew that she'd done it. Her words continued, quiet but deadly, "It's kind of Dr Rapace to make me an offer, but I wonder if I could tell you what I would love to be able to do? Although it would be nice to continue as manager in a surgery, I think I am ready for a change. I have a little money saved and I wonder if I could tempt you. Forgive me, I know it's all a bit of a hurry but in truth I have always wanted to do this. I wonder if I can count on your support, Dr Binder?"

Her oleaginous tones continued and right on cue he, once again, did her bidding and swallowed just about every false line she fed to him. In so doing he assured not only his own obliteration but also that of those, every single one, who were trying to help him.

He was putty in her hands. She did her best to suppress her triumphant smile modulated by pure wickedness, but ultimately she realised her days of concealment were now over. Put simply, nothing and no one could stop her now. More than this, she then looked into the distance, the triumph that existed on her face in that moment like that of a captain who had just weathered her ship brilliantly so as to outmanoeuvre her pursuers. Astern of her as she looked back over the taffrail lay the daft, the destitute, the dispossessed – and those soon to drown.

Her work was done and her success was now guaranteed. She turned her back to him as she hugged the papers to her chest as if only she recognised their true value. Her smug, self-satisfied grin was now modulated by triumph and the certain knowledge that her position was now impregnable.

Dr Binder was still speaking to her, but she left his room without either looking at him or looking back. She didn't even bother to close his door.

For a day or two the surgery would continue as if nothing had happened. This would be only for the shortest of times. Quite simply, nothing could avert the catastrophe that was about to be inflicted on the small surgery and everyone within.

Petunia finished her shift and prepared to walk up the long lane to the bus stop. She had seen a prescription for Mrs Spencer and had asked one of the locums to sign it.

She knocked on the back door. Bobby, the large ginger tom looked at her suspiciously and scurried past her as she approached. One or two other cats snoozed on the veranda completely unaffected by her approach. Mrs Spencer came to the door and opened it slowly at first and then with more enthusiasm as she welcomed her young visitor. Petunia stepped back as the door swung outwards. "Come in, Petunia, is it? How are things, my dear? Have you settled in? I have seen the paper, things look really awful and you have only just been taken on. Are you going to be all right? Poor Dr Binder, nothing seems to go right for that man. I was hoping things would improve for him."

Matilda looked very sad as the bright glow that seemed to emanate from her became dull and subdued.

"We don't really know anything. Mrs Spencer. So many rumours are going round that the CCG are going to close the surgery and distribute all the patients to local surgeries. We are just trying to get through each day and help the patients as best we can. Poor Dr Binder looks dreadful. I wish I could help him, but it's hard to know how. Anyway, I hope you don't mind, but I saw your prescription on the top of the pile and thought you'd like me to pop round with it as I was walking past anyway."

Matilda drew strength from the cheery manner and smile that lay under the younger woman's long fringe and she brightened infectiously.

She motioned to Petunia to come inside, initially holding the door open but then suddenly turning away from her visitor in order to quickly close the door to her front room.

Petunia was a little puzzled by the rapidity of the movement from the elderly lady which seemed at variance with her typically slow and methodical moves but didn't think anything of it until much later. Matilda sensed the young woman's puzzlement and offered, as embarrassment overcame her, that she didn't like the cats going in her front room, which was the room she kept for best. Petunia nodded good-naturedly.

Matilda took her through to the back room. This, judging by its careworn appearance and the stronger feline odour, was obviously where the older lady spent much of her time. The little gas fire was on and laboured erratically but successfully against the prevailing winds coming off the moors. The atmosphere had become a little dry and stuffy, which made Petunia feel uncomfortable, but she smiled reflexly as she sat on the settee that the older lady had indicated.

"Yes, I don't know what's going to become of poor Dr Binder. I have known him for so long and, of course, his family. It was absolutely tragic what happened to his wife and son that terrible day. He'd always been a fabulous, caring doctor but, sadly, things changed that day." She pointed to the open newspaper on the table, "It says there that he is going to lose his surgery and that they will disperse all the patients. I read a few weeks ago that his partner, Dr Rapace, has put a planning application in on the old cinema in the centre of Horwich. He is converting it to consulting rooms for a new surgery. Have you heard anything about that, Petunia?"

"No, Mrs Spencer, I have heard nothing about this from either of the doctors, although Dr Rapace very rarely speaks to the staff. Come to think of it he rarely speaks to Dr Binder. No doubt we'll soon find out what's happening, though I wish I could help Dr Binder in some way. Everyone who knows him says the same thing – what a kind, caring doctor he was and how much he changed after the accident."

"I am sure a clever girl like you will find a way of helping him, my dear."

Petunia looked at her watch. "Oh my, I'd better be going. It's nice to see you again, Mrs Spencer. Oh, I nearly forgot; I found out what that noise was that you can hear at night. I think they've been moving some heavy machinery past here late at night. I should have more information soon and, if so, perhaps I could pop back and let you know?"

"Of course, my dear, any time and perhaps next time stay and have a nice cuppa with me?"

"I'll look forward to that, Mrs Spencer. Good bye."

Matilda showed her to the door and Petunia walked back up the lane, as the wind seemed to propel her forwards, to see if the little car was waiting for her.

The newly-promoted senior reporter of the *Horwich Chronicle* had driven down the lane some minutes before Petunia's arrival. He'd been told what time the receptionist had finished her shift and had parked his black Toyota in the surgery car park. He'd followed her up the lane and also seen her enter the old lady's house. Her back was to him the whole time and he didn't really get a look at her face. He could see the masses of unruly hair being swept by the breeze but this served as more of a distraction rather than a means to his discovering the receptionist's identity. He'd brought his camera and was hoping to get a good picture of her. He walked slowly but otherwise directly behind her. The large ginger tom arched his back and spat at him as he approached. The reporter lashed out with his right leg but missed the large cat which immediately ran into some bushes. He waited patiently.

There was something about that walk; he'd seen that traipsing gait somewhere before and although the shock of hair hid much of her face and obscured her eyes, this too seemed familiar. No further answers came to him at that point, so he simply continued to watch from his concealed vantage point. He realised that it was only a matter of time before she re-appeared and at that time he would be ready.

Some time later, he was rewarded by the opening of the door and he could see the receptionist coming out. Although he was poised with his camera, having de-activated the flash, as she left the house he no longer needed to capture her picture. The moment she appeared and turned on the veranda a gust of wind caught the fringe and swept it up and over her forehead. He held his camera but was otherwise frozen to the spot. His mouth fell open with the shock, for he now knew exactly who she was. He knew, too, in that second that the plans of Ms Makepeace had been thrown into disarray.

The presence of this person was certainly very bad news for his source, just as it had been for him the last time they had met. He was barely able to contain himself for the few minutes as she walked up the track to meet up with the little car that was waiting for her by the bus stop. A rare event then took place; his hands started shaking as he dabbed at the number of Ms Makepeace and as it rang he held the phone to his left ear.

"Yes?" she snapped irritably.

"I know, I know who she is and she's trouble."

"I take it," she began acidly, "that you are referring to our new receptionist?" Having demonstrated her lack of interest and now the irrelevance of whoever she was, she continued.

"I very much doubt that she will pose any threat to me; nothing I can't handle, in any event."

"Look, I've seen what this bitch can do and I think you are in danger." The reporter then spent the next five minutes in a long diatribe against Petunia Mumple and also recounted in some detail how, in their previous dealings, she'd outfoxed him at every turn. The reporter was breathless as he finished, having poured out as much information as he could, and there was a long delay before Ms Makepeace, having continued to eat her dinner as he went on, detected the silence.

"I doubt that, somehow. But at least I know my suspicions about her are correct."

"Look, I wouldn't underestimate her, and I wouldn't go up against her."

Amanda Makepeace then laughed, with a titillated but certainly unconcerned air.

"Oh, I suspect she's the one who's underestimated me, and as for going up against her, then, maybe she should not have become involved. In any event I don't think she'll cause me much of a problem; it's a bit late for that. In point of fact, it's time we rid ourselves, once and for all, of this nuisance."

"All's I'm saying is don't take your eyes off her, watch her like a hawk. I'll be keepin' my eye on her, for sure. She's big trouble, trust me."

"Trust *me*, I'll be watching her like a hawk all right, as a hawk watches a field mouse," she laughed again. "Thank you for your *warning,*" she offered facetiously.

She put the phone down and took a deep mouthful of the excellent red she'd opened to have with her meal. It tasted no less pleasant than when she'd started. The interfering girl couldn't even dispel her enjoyment of her wine which could only be seen as a good omen.

In any event, she'd done her best to display her indifference to all things regarding the new girl. However, she did allow herself just the merest hint of relief, certainly more than she could admit to anyone including herself, at the fact that she'd pushed her plans forward in the way that she had. Having finished the bottle of wine she poured herself a generous G&T and raised the tall glass to herself. It looked as though the receptionist was about to join the ranks of those who'd dared to go up against Amanda Makepeace; for sure, their skeletons were scattered to a man, or woman, in her wake as she moved ever onwards like a force that could neither be checked nor resisted.

Amanda was a formidable opponent and would fight tooth and nail until she'd got her own way. Sadly, her vanquished opponents would often be totally and gratuitously destroyed. Very few went up against her and remained intact to fight another day. She was particularly cruel with those who'd had the temerity to challenge her and a particularly damning fate awaited those who did so. She prepared such a fate for Petunia as she quietly sipped her gin and tonic.

In addition to preparing a suitable punishment for the bogus but hapless receptionist, Amanda also sent off several e-mails. The longest of these was to her boss, Felix. So delighted was he with the contents of the e-mail, he telephoned her as soon as he had digested its content.

"Amanda Makepeace, what a marvel you are. You see, this is why I tell the board that you are worth every penny of what we pay you and that you also earn those rather large bonuses we pay you for a successful outcome." Felix thought for a moment, trying to remember a time when she'd not either triumphed or collected her bonus. He could not recollect a time when she'd not done both of these things. "That was a brilliant move, Mandy, just how did you think of it?"

"Well, I reasoned that if the funds would not be in place for a week or two, then we'd be vulnerable. Anyone who got wind of our plans who either had, or could raise, significant funds, or had suitable investors, could frustrate us at the last moment, just when everything is coming together. Then it struck me that there was a simple way of protecting our position even though funding will be delayed."

"So how much did it cost you?"

"It's ours for £75,000, and I made sure it was signed and sealed."

Felix laughed uncontrollably how he loved a bargain. "75k! What a miracle worker you are. It might interest you to know that the board gave you leave to go up to a million."

"A million! You see, that is why you need me; I get you the assets you need and make sure everything goes to plan even when there's been an unforeseen delay."

"No argument from me on this one, Mandy. You've saved us a fortune."

"I suppose you could always put the difference in my bonus pot."

"I think if this deal goes through, you'll get that and more. This is *that* big a deal, I am sure I don't have to tell you."

"Well, I'm just glad I've not spent months working among these absolute losers for nothing! I can't wait to get out of here and be among some real people."

"It won't be long now, thanks to you. Hang in there for a few more days and we'll be all done."

"Okay then, lover, I'd better go and make sure the trap I've sprung for our new nosy receptionist is all in place."

"Remind me never to upset you, won't you."

Suddenly her eyes darkened, "Now, that would be a grave mistake. See you soon. Night, night."

CHAPTER X

Tender Trap

The following day, Ms Makepeace appeared in reception with a full tray of doughnuts; one for each member of staff. Much more than this, she was pleasant, lingered in the office, and even spoke to several of the receptionists rather than simply barking out orders and heaping opprobrium upon all who should come within her gaze. The girls were amazed at the transformation in the manager. One or two even dared to think that she had turned over a new leaf. Perhaps the problems facing the surgery had had a positive influence upon her. The least perceptive even began to believe that things might improve.

"Petunia, be a dear and get my mobile phone would you? I believe I left it on my desk."

Petunia's mouth opened with incredulity. Sadly, although she remained highly suspicious, she was unable to guess the trap that lay in wait: a trap that was about to destroy her.

She dutifully went upstairs and entered the manager's office. She quickly identified the mobile phone. She saw that it was perched on an open official-looking document. She immediately knew what the document was and just how important it was. She knew in that second this was a vital piece of information. Moreover, the advantage that this gave her was fleeting; she had to act on her new found knowledge immediately.

'Application for Carob Oil and Gas to bid for exploration rights on the West Pennine Moors.' She quickly scanned the document. Carob Oil had obviously been testing the ground and had discovered large quantities of shale oil and gas and had prepared a bid to formalise their preliminary findings with a firm offer of £160 million.

Petunia grabbed Amanda's phone and knew in that moment what she had to do if she were to save the surgery and everyone who worked there. She had to act fast if she were to stand a chance of stopping her.

She returned the phone to the manager who waited patiently for the first time in her life for the receptionist to bring it to her. As she accepted it with a smile rather than the usual snarl, all present should have guessed that she was waiting for far more than a mobile phone – and it had just been placed within her reach.

The off-white mini was waiting for Petunia as she left work. She began to speak as soon as she entered the car. "Just as we suspected, Ms Makepeace has a far bigger game in play. As you discovered, she works for an oil and gas company who are bidding for the fracking rights. There is a fortune below ground and they have assessed how much and what it's worth," she nodded behind her.

"And so, how does this affect the surgery?"

"You said it yourself. The surgery closes, they then move in. They have bid £160 million."

"Wow, that's a lot of money. Don't even think what I think you are thinking," his mouth dried and his speech became hoarse as he swallowed.

"How do you know what I am thinking?"

"I always know what you are thinking, especially when you are about to commit funds, and in this case massive funds, to help others."

"Yes, and we have to outbid Carob Oil."

"Outbid them, why should we do this?"

"Look, you know why. It's the only way to save the surgery. Ms Makepeace has no interest whatsoever in the surgery continuing. Her every move has been to destroy it.

She was just waiting for presumably positive results from their test well, or whatever they do, before they put a firm bid in. They are now ready to move. What's more I read a letter on her desk. Carob Oil and Gas will have finance in place in the next two days."

"That settles it! Surely, it's way over our heads. As I suspected, they must have some serious backers if they have access to that sort of money. We can't take on an oil company for heaven's sake. I am very nervous about going anywhere near this. You know how badly the surgery is performing. I am not sure it can be saved even if there were no fracking."

"I agree it's a much bigger deal than we are used to, but don't you think it's the same as we always do but with more noughts on the end?"

He coughed, desperately trying to regain his voice against his throat now like parchment. "Those noughts could sink your finances, forever. Those noughts will have you in the poor house. Those noughts will ruin you." She held his hand, "Yes, yes, I get the picture about those noughts. Besides, ruin *us*, as I have told you before."

"Ruin is still ruin no matter how many you share it with! My darling, some things you just have to let go. I don't think this is our fight somehow. Perhaps we should just let the surgery die. You've done your best. You've done all that a girl could do. Walk away now and we move on. We'll find so many other deserving cases to help."

"No, look, what are we doing here? Why have we come this far, if we are to quit now?"

He didn't think this at all, he knew this was not their fight and intervening was fraught with danger. He just had to continue to try and convince her. "But, my love, this is *too* far. I just have a bad feeling about it."

"We have to save them, I promised."

"No, you didn't. You received a letter, from a person or persons whom we do not know. It could be Amanda

Makepeace for all you know. You came, you saw, you did all you could; and now it's time to leave."

At that moment, she didn't speak; she just looked at him with the large, blue eyes that seemed even larger in such moments. He knew with one glance, like a magic spell, the argument was lost. He knew, perhaps he'd known all along, that she'd just have to follow the path to its logical conclusion. This was her way and he suspected that neither word nor deed from him would change her. At least he'd warned her and, strangely, by delivering such a warning, it calmed his own anxiety, bordering on panic.

"You know if you commit funds to this it will consume all you have?"

"I've told you it's all *we* have."

"And there is no guarantee of any sort of return. Perhaps we should just let it go. The CCG will appoint others to take on the patients."

"But what about all those we promised? All those I promised?"

"Promises can only go so far."

"No, I can't accept that, promises go as far as we are able. We go all the way. And as for return, there never has been any return that mattered other than saving people."

He knew, then, this is what drove her and he could no more persuade her to change her mind than change her shoe size. He accepted her argument gracefully, as always.

"Very well then, I can see you are determined."

He knew this is what made her so special; she knew when to cut away the cold logic and let a very different set of emotions take the field. He smiled and kissed her.

"I promise not to say I told you so."

"Okay, tomorrow I phone Mr Bloor and we go in. Agreed?"

"Agreed," he kissed her again.

Neither his wakefulness all through the night, nor the fleeting moments of sleep he caught gave him any release as he turned over their strategy again and again. The morning light brought no further comfort. Moreover, although he'd done his best to lie perfectly still as he'd gone through the night so as not to wake her, he suspected that she'd done exactly the same.

The following morning the bank manager, Mr Bloor, advised caution.

"I can detect that you are most keen to go forward with this project, my dear. You know that the bank will continue to extend to you every facility. This single deal, however, will render your account fully depleted and though there will, as always, be due to you some interest payments, these are of an inconsequential nature compared to the sum you are about to transact. I've had a look at Carob Oil, they have significant borrowings and are highly geared. They will need this project to generate income for them fairly soon. Any sort of delay may well put significant pressure on their financial viability. It's cost them an awful lot already to get the site survey done and to calculate the likely gas and oil yield. They have to make this pay and I am sure you will realise that as they are committed they will throw funds at it in the hope that they can bring a return sooner rather than later. The smart move may well be to wait; keep one's powder dry, so to speak."

She listened carefully to all that he had to say, just as she always did. She thanked him with effortless charm and good grace, just as she always did. His heart skipped a beat, in talking to her, just as it always did. Finally, at the end of their conversation, the manager knew that his duty was done. He knew, too, that she had set her heart on going forward and there were no further words he could offer that would make her change her mind nor could he convey the words that he wanted to shout to her; to beg her in words he knew that he could never voice.

"Very well then, my dear. May I say that in the time that I have known you, I have marvelled at the wonderful things you have done for so many people. I can only hope that there are many more that you will go on to help. If you lose, however, and lose now, as I suspect there is great danger in your so doing, then all this will come to an end and you'll be lucky to retain your residence in Canada."

"I'm aware of that, Mr Bloor."

"So be it. I am here to fulfil your instructions and I have always been honoured to have done so. I am in awe of you," his voice started breaking up, he corrected his own words quickly, "of the kind and far-reaching projects that you have undertaken. I suspected you'd say that. I have done my duty and warned you of the perilous nature of these current events and the transaction you are about to make."

"I thank you, Mr Bloor, for your sage counsel and kind words and especially for all that you have done for me over the past many months."

He knew that his words had run out and so had those of this remarkable young woman. He typed a few instructions and within seconds of his doing so £180 million one hundred, which represented an overarching offer, was made to the owners to buy the fracking and drilling rights to their piece of land, that nestled in that windy valley just down from the surgery.

Within minutes of this conversation, and following instructions from their client, the offer was accepted and the transaction became irrevocable. By the time it was keyed, and the correct safeguards had been put in place, not quite two minutes from start to finish had elapsed. This was all the time required to ruin someone.

The manager gulped and hoped that she did not hear the involuntary noise as he did so; he was used to handling much bigger funds than this and normally did so without missing a breath. And yet, now, in talking to this wonderful young woman who'd selflessly helped so many, he couldn't help but feel nothing short of terrified on her behalf. His hands were sweaty and they trembled like those of a teenager stealing his first kiss. He had to work hard on his voice so that it appeared with its usual calm and deep tones rather than the squeaky timbre that he suspected would have come forth.

"It's done. The money has been transferred and accepted. The paperwork will come through in a few days but the transaction can no longer be reversed. It only remains for me," and his voice now trembled, like his hands, as he continued, "for me to wish you the very best of fortune, my dear."

"Thank you, Archibald, you are most kind as always. Thank you and goodbye. I will keep you informed."

He replaced his handset, and suddenly felt very old.

Petunia could only think, as she terminated the call, that she'd done the right thing. She knew she'd done the right thing, just as she always tried to do. Without doubt, she was now in control of the situation and could protect the surgery and Matilda Spencer too. As soon as Ms Makepeace was out of the way, and surely now that things were over there'd be no reason for her to stay as much as a minute longer, then Petunia could approach the CCG and the CCA and beg for a stay of execution. For sure, things could, from this point on, only improve and the dark days were over. However, a tiny thought, somewhere deep within, like an oil leak in a precision and high-revving engine, begged to disagree. She could feel its restless presence on every thought she had that afternoon. It had been too easy; surely Ms Makepeace would not leave a document of such importance lying open on her desk. It was at this point that the tiny thought achieved a much greater momentum within; now bordering on panic. For Petunia knew, somehow deep inside, that the dark days were about to become even darker. So much so, she now wondered if she would ever see the dawn.

The fate that awaited her was revealed a little later the same day. She received an urgent phone call from her confidante.

"I have just obtained the report carried out by the drone survey company. They were delayed getting the drone airborne because of the extreme wind. They've only just come back to me now."

"And, yes, go on," she held her breath, knowing, somehow, that disaster lay in his next words.

"The site has no *access* without that surgery. They need that land and without it the whole resource is worth *nothing*. You have to buy that surgery and it has to be done today. I can only hope that we are not too late. It's the only way to protect your investment. It's the only way to maintain control. The surgery, and its car park, represent the key that unlocks the whole puzzle. This is why she is here. They've applied for temporary access to allow them some test drillings. These are the tracks that you've seen for the test drill holes. I suspect Amanda Makepeace installed herself here so as to make sure they could get on and off the land beyond the car park. She needs to own that land as well as close the surgery. Land that is suddenly worth a lot of money – provided they can get access to it."

She silenced the call and stared off into the distance. The restless feeling that she had in the pit of her stomach continued to gnaw away at her, making her feel nervous, nauseous and also full of foreboding. She knew that such feelings would not depart until she'd purchased the surgery and its land. Without this she'd just spent all she had on a patch of moorland that was, by itself, worthless.

Moreover, Dr Binder wasn't in the surgery. Two locums had been retained to see the patients. The whole place had a restless feel to it. Nobody seemed to know anything. Even Amanda Makepeace made only a brief appearance. Shortly after Petunia had terminated her phone call, she saw the manager's BMW powering up the hill. The loose stones and asphalt, that was breaking up, were churned up further by her rear tyres as she drove aggressively up the long slope. As the locums got on with the surgeries, Dr Rapace finished his morning session. He put in a brief appearance in the office while he signed some prescriptions. Petunia noticed that he appeared brighter than his usual taciturn self and although he ignored everyone as he signed the pile in front of him, he gave a little whistle as he applied himself to the job in hand. Shortly after this he, too, left for the day while the locums continued.

How Petunia managed to wait until the end of the day she would never know. As soon as her shift finished she left through the double office doors and went a little way up the hill where an off-white Mini, that was not new but was in excellent condition, waited for her.

Sincere, open and honest brown eyes studied her carefully as she got in. She turned away from their concerned gaze. He kissed her quickly and it didn't need close scrutiny for him to detect the nervousness that was applied to her face, and also that she was doing her best to control her trembling as she sat in the passenger seat.

CHAPTER XI

Ruin

He started the engine without speaking as he knew she'd want to get over to Dr Binder's without delay. Few words were exchanged as he drove. Without doubt the same words were running through both their minds anyway. Both occupants displayed the air of two prisoners about to be led down to face a firing squad. Eventually they reached their destination. He parked a little way from the GP's house.

"Would you like me to come in with you?" he managed to say despite his dry throat that made speech a little uncomfortable.

"No, I'd better do this alone," she replied. "I won't be long," she added with the tremor from her hands now extending to her voice.

She got out of the car and looked up. The grey, overcast day with its persistent wind began to give up its efforts to shed light as night rushed to claim what was left of the miserable day for its own. Although he'd stopped a little way off, the headlights remained on and they illuminated the path down to the small, detached, stone cottage that had been denied for years even basic upkeep and repairs. It looked in a sorry state as it stood against the bleak moorland, especially in the darkness that now seemed to envelop it. Not only the cottage but the garden, too, gave off an air of neglect as though once keen and interested owners had departed with nobody moving in to replace them.

Petunia saw a child's swing in the garden, its colourful paint now peeling and the once bright chain supporting the plastic seat now almost worn through with rust.

Dr Binder came to the door after a delay as she tapped, having given up on the non-functioning bell a minute or two before. He looked with a slight hint of recognition as he set eyes on her but did not seem unduly surprised to see her. His movements were both slow and quiet almost to the point of displaying a shuffling gait. His features looked pale and grey and seemed to blend with the night. More than this, it seemed that he was now more of a ghost; maintaining a presence while no longer occupying what had been a loving family home – clearly some years ago.

Her reflex smile was returned by a simple nod although he tried to pitch some warmth in his words. "Ah, Petunia isn't it? Welcome. Why are you here so late?" Although he asked the questions, he'd already sensed why she was on his doorstep.

"Hello, Dr Binder. I do hope you can forgive me for appearing at your home in this way? I have something of crucial importance to discuss with you. Could you spare me a minute or two of your time?"

He nearly laughed at this point, as he thought that time was one thing he still held in abundance. Indeed, each day it seemed to pass more slowly. It was apparent that very soon his days would be filled with the sensation of even more time – with which he could now do nothing.

He offered no further words but did his best to assume a smile on his tired face and simply nodded as he indicated that she should step inside against the dark, the biting cold and the wind. Although his hall was illuminated, the single bulb made little impact against the overall gloom that seemed even worse in the house than she'd experienced walking towards the cottage in the beam of the car headlights.

She shivered a little as he led her through the cottage and into the dark and untidy reception room. He switched on a standard lamp, but the tired and dusty shade defeated the efforts of the low-wattage bulb and little further light appeared in the murky room.

She sat down on the small sofa which sagged even under her insubstantial weight. She took a deep breath but otherwise her words began at once.

"Dr Binder, I have some information for you. I have discovered that there is a much bigger plan in play here. It involves the surgery, but really only the land that the surgery sits upon. The steep-sided valley that lies beyond the car park is rich in oil and probably gas. Ms Makepeace, I believe, is really working for an oil and gas fracking company that plans to exploit that resource. In order to reach it they need your surgery. As I am sure you will realise the land is worth a fortune but not without the surgery land, including the car park. I have stalled her plans for now but I wonder if you would permit me to purchase the surgery from you. Or at least, please don't sell it until you've had time to look at what I am saying. This will give us time until we can decide what is best for all concerned and especially the surgery."

He looked steadily at Petunia. His expression had regret engraved more than usual on his sad features and his speech was delayed for so long as to make the young woman unsettled. As it was, this was for good reason. Even at this late hour, in the gloom of his living room he could not fail to see the enthusiasm that ran across the bright features of the young receptionist.

She was about to fill the void with more speech, but the GP raised his hand to slow the excitement that her frame could barely contain, for he knew he was about to impart bad news.

"I can't sell you the surgery, Petunia, much as I would want to."

The bright expression on her face was plummeting even as the words came forth, "May I ask why, Dr Binder?"

"I cannot sell what I no longer own."

She saw it all then, the fate that awaited her.

"You sold it, Dr Binder? To Amanda?" She just had to

clarify what the worst of nightmares could only reveal to her as her expression continued, now into the pit of despair.

"Yes, she approached me yesterday. She wants to open a school for disadvantaged children on the site of the surgery." Even as he spoke the words he knew that he was simply reiterating lies that he'd been fed. "At least, that's what she *said*." His expression seemed even more sad, if such a thing were possible.

"A school for disadvantaged children?" she repeated as if she had not quite heard the words. Moreover, just repeating them made her want to laugh hysterically. She then coughed as if she had just inhaled something very unfamiliar, but toxic, as the truth hit her. "You sold, Amanda the surgery?" she managed to say although her voice was so hoarse with shock and disbelief that she could barely complete the question.

"I am sorry about this, Petunia. It seems we have both been outmanoeuvred." He could see that Petunia was still too shocked to be able to manage more words just at that time.

He seemed both surprised and betrayed in equal measure. His words in any case were redundant ones.

"So, you are saying that Amanda won't be opening a school there?"

She remained incapable of any speech for the moment, let alone summoning the strength to confirm what was patently clear. In the event, so many other things started flooding through her brain and all of them pointed to a low water mark of disasters. She simply nodded by way of an affirmative. She realised, however, that she needed to ask a still more pressing question.

"Have you signed a *contract*, Dr Binder?"

"Yes, Fergus Rapace told me that he is leaving and setting up a new surgery. He plans to take over the patient list. He went behind my back and has put a bid in to the CCA to provide General Medical Services to the entire list. He acted as witness to the papers that Amanda had drawn up. Actually had them in her hand, come to think of it." His sense of betrayal had already reached a low point; there was no further for such an emotion to fall.

Petunia gulped very hard. Words could no longer change the situation whether she were capable of speech or otherwise. Her future and the destruction that ran with it, however, appeared to be rampaging through her head. Her investment was worth nothing; what was more, *she* was worth nothing. She could certainly no longer guarantee the survival of the surgery: in point of fact her intervention had guaranteed its destruction. Even worse than this, Mrs Spencer's house was situated at the entrance to what would soon become a busy and noisy construction and drilling site. She determined that, come what may, she must prevent this, even if she ended up penniless. At least she could still block that.

More than this, she had been comprehensively outmanoeuvred by a cleverer and far more dangerous opponent than she'd realised. Dr Binder sensed all too easily her shock and pain like that of a person now drowning in freezing water. Her mouth opened and closed as if she were gasping for the last dregs of air her body would ever inhale.

"No, Dr Binder, I suspect that a school is not what she has in mind," she offered as some of her composure returned.

"You may be aware that the CCA are planning to close me down. The *Horwich Chronicle* got hold of the story and released it, thereby directly contravening the conditions that were attached to the CCA's offer of a period of grace, pending an appeal. I don't know how…" his voice now trailed off but his level of understanding went up. "I think I am beginning to see. I suppose at least the patients will have a GP when Dr Rapace opens in the old cinema."

"I suspect, Dr Binder, that the patients to a man, woman or child would rather have you."

He smiled as he acknowledged her genuine kindness.

"It appears that they have both been plotting against me. That is why she came, simply to get her hands on that land."

"It appears so, Dr Binder."

"People tried to tell me and I wouldn't listen. Tina Bessemer, the previous office manager, begged me to open my eyes."

His gaze now seemed even more vacant and far away before suddenly a new enquiry formed on his expression. He focussed on the young woman, the one who'd tried to save him. "But why is this of interest to you? I can see that you are not just a receptionist."

She forced a smile, a more depleted version of the one that visited her face so readily. "As I told you, Dr Binder, I am just someone who wanted to help. Someone who was trying to protect and preserve the surgery."

"And I let you down. I let them all down."

"Don't be too hard on yourself, Dr Binder. Sometimes things go against us and get away from us despite our best efforts and intentions." She would lose count of the number of times she would say these exact words to herself in the days ahead.

"Is there anything we can do?"

"I'm not sure at this point. I suspect it's no longer our move. We will hear more, I think, in the next day or two."

"I knew it, or I should have known. You are rather more than just a receptionist."

"No, not really, Dr Binder, I guess I am just a receptionist, after all. And not that there's anything wrong with that."

She rose to go, feeling much more apprehensive than when she'd arrived. Any hope had been transmuted from precious thoughts to leaden ones.

"What are you going to do next, Petunia?"

"I think it's time for a haircut, Dr Binder."

She was about to head out from the room, but chose to move back towards him, just as he stood. She was about to shake his hand but as she approached she could not resist hugging him; the first warm touch he'd experienced in over five years. He touched his cheek carefully as she turned to leave.

She did her best to cover the depth of misery that now ran through her. He could not fail to see the sadness that was a reflection of what he had recognised within himself for so long. Moreover, he knew this to be the path that his own unhappiness had signposted for him; and it seemed, now, for others too. She left, the sadness making each footfall seem more heavy and agonising as the dark enveloped her.

The tall man with the honest, deep-brown eyes waited for her as she came towards him. The car headlights remained on but he had, got out of the car. He'd waited for her just outside the cottage.

The wind swept by so forcefully that under ordinary conditions he'd have been chilled to the bone as he waited. And yet, things were far from ordinary. Ordinary was when things had gone well: people had been helped and they'd quietly withdrawn to go and find, and to help, others who were no less worthy or in need of that help. Now, all at once, things were extra-ordinary and with that excursion from the normal had come total loss. He could see by her very bearing that things had gone badly for them. Most likely, too, as he'd foreseen and Mr Bloor had warned, they faced ruin.

On the other side of the cottage Dr Binder stared out of the window for some time. He continued to stare although he could see very little in the darkness. And yet, just at that moment, he could hear the children play. Children playing, as young ones should, running in the garden or in the playground. These were the same children, he now realised, that he heard the night his wife and son died, killed entirely by his careless incompetence.

Without doubt, he deserved this fate, but surely others, ones who'd depended on him, did not; those trusting souls who had supported him and backed him and, as it would seem, had staked everything in so doing. He accepted that he had let everyone down, all those around him, all those who hoped for better times. Those, too, who'd waited and begged and prayed for him to forgive himself as, no doubt, would his wife and little boy.

Dr Binder sat there for some time. He could still hear the children. He knew, somehow, that he would, once more, hear the sound of those children at play the day he died. It felt within that it should be today. Petunia, Tina and others had been right all along. He could see it now so clearly. Just how had he missed so much?

The brutal truth followed soon after. He knew exactly why he'd missed so much. People had got on with their own nefarious activities whilst he had been unable to see past the photo on his desk and had been unable to feel anything other than the gold ring on his left hand – as well as the loss it represented. His clarity of thought had come too late. He was now incapable of saving himself let alone the surgery. His livelihood had passed to his former partner and, he'd believed, friend and there was nothing he could do to change the situation.

After some further thoughts of bitter self-recrimination, he got up to turn the light off. He sat, once again, but now in total darkness: he couldn't bear to see his own reflection in the dark windows. The sound made by the children had now stopped but he looked anyway to confirm what he already knew.

Petunia ran to the tall man who'd waited for her. One who would always wait, for however long it took and no matter how dreadful the news. He kissed her but said nothing. He knew that at that moment whatever words he'd assembled would be inadequate. The couple walked slowly back towards the Mini. He placed a long arm around her shoulders like a scarf against the wind. He simply waited for her to speak.

"I was too late. Dr Binder has already sold the surgery to Amanda. She told him that she plans to open a school there for disadvantaged children. He *believed* her and signed the contract there and then; the one that she just happened to have on her. Dr Rapace, as ever, was eager to act as witness. Wow, with friends and partners like these, the poor soul didn't stand a chance. There's nothing I can do. We are ruined. You were right. Mr Bloor warned me. I should have listened to you; to you both."

He held her, sensing that the tears were but a moment away.

"Look, you did what you thought was for the best, as always. You tried to help as many as you could."

"And look where it's led us; we are ruined."

"Not so. We have our youth and a full life that has never depended on your money. We will do something else. We always knew it wasn't forever. You always said that." His voice went up a register as he did his best to inject optimism into the gloom that was all-pervading as the wind whipped around them with an intensity bordering on pain.

"I just didn't expect it to all come crashing down on one foolish move. How stupid I've been."

He was just about to refute her words and replace them with much warmer and more accurate ones of his own. However, just as he was about to open the car, the tears that he'd been anticipating began. This was a rare occurrence for her. They led bright active lives but he knew, as soon as he saw her approach, that today was altogether different. She'd probably never cried so much, except perhaps on the day she'd lost her parents in that terrible fire. Even then, as a youngster, she may not have appreciated the sorrow that surrounded her as the fireman wept as he held her while his colleagues went in over and over again attempting to pull her parents out but failing on each occasion. Well, she was weeping now, silently at first and then the convulsive sobs hit her.

In fact her suffering now was immeasurable and if the wind had not raised itself to the most penetrating of gales, the heavens would have wept too. She thought about her unremitting sadness when, as a little girl, she'd gone to live with her aunt, knowing only that her mummy and daddy had been taken to heaven by the angels who'd found them in the fire. Now, however, her pain displayed very different attributes. All he could do was to hold her, as he would continue to do until the mountains had dissolved into the sea, if need be.

Her own thoughts were the most unforgiving. She'd failed, this was patently clear. The failure she could cope with: she'd failed before. She'd learnt from each of those times. It wasn't even so much her pride that had been wounded, although she had to admit that this had more than a little to do with her disquiet.

Ultimately, she accepted that she'd been outwitted and out-manoeuvred by another. One who'd used, perhaps, devious and unkind means but nevertheless, perfectly permissible ones. What hurt her the most were the motives displayed in the way in which her vanquisher had conducted herself: ones that rested on greed, bullying, intimidation and lies in order to bring about her advantage.

Petunia had known for so many years, having lost her parents, how unfair the world could be. She'd reasoned that, although such a thing could never, ever be described as 'fair', perhaps this was simply the random nature of the dispassionate working of the cosmic tumblers as they fell into line, causing misery as they did so.

She would never expect benign conditions and sunny days just because she'd used her wealth unceasingly for the good of others. She knew that she had no right or expectation that she was in some way deserving as a result.

This was it, however, the bare and stark truth; her failure now was solely due to her mistake. Her poor calculation and hasty moves had led her here, to this point. By intervening too soon, and in the wrong way, she'd not only brought about self ruin but she'd also terminated her chances of continuing her philanthropy in the future. Others had seen the mistake she was about to commit to; why hadn't she?

Yes, she'd learnt, always, always, by the mistakes she'd made. In so doing she came back improved and stronger. On this occasion she'd been so signally outmanoeuvred that her chances of recovery were next to none. Her financial wherewithal had imploded with her own rashness.

Moreover, she had to admit that this more than hinted at her real failure. Perhaps, in fact definitely, she'd become complacent. On so many occasions, deal after deal had been completed flawlessly, safely and for the sole benefit of others. Perhaps she'd assumed that, because she was at all times striving to help others, she could do no wrong. The cosmic tumblers had begged to differ.

The other point that she had to accept was that perhaps pride had had more to do with her fall than she'd been hitherto able to admit. Amanda Makepeace had simply used this against her and this, more than anything, was why it hurt so much. Now, having been vanquished in this way, she'd be lucky to keep the house in Canada. Her tears were for the life she'd lost as well as for those she'd be unable to help in the future.

On the occasions in the past when she'd been wrong, and especially when it was her fault, her aunt had encouraged her to pursue a simple but painful strategy. She ran through this now. Firstly, to admit one's error and assume responsibility for it. Secondly, to apologise. Finally, to limit the damage as far as possible. She knew in that moment that she would use the best of her abilities and what remained of her resources to do this now.

She wiped away her tears; feeling sorry for herself was definitely not on the list.

He detected her brightening mood. "Fancy that, a school for the disadvantaged. What a woman! So, what do we do now?"

"Well, as I told Dr Binder, it's time to get my hair cut. We then move on."

"Sounds good to me." He turned out one of his pockets. "I have a fiver here if that's any use?"

"Always, always a good start. I guess we are half way there already." She kissed him as they entered the Mini. Both suddenly realised that they were very cold. He fired the engine and switched the heater to maximum before he drove them away.

CHAPTER XII

Press Conference

The following day Amanda Makepeace had called a press conference. News cameras from both ITV and the BBC had made the short journey to the Media City studios at Salford Quays. Ms Makepeace had kept them all waiting for a few minutes before triumphantly striding in. Her sharp heels almost cutting into the carpet, they could feel her approach by her very heavy footfalls even before they could see her. Moreover, she gave off a confident celebratory air as she came forward, like a gladiator about to be feted as the champion over all comers.

"Ladies, gentlemen, thank you for coming. I wanted to tell you about the exciting plans that the company I work for, Carob Oil and Gas, have for the West Pennine moors."

One of the reporters interrupted her. She stared daggers at him.

"Yes, we've been hearing this for some time but nobody has ever found a way to get the heavy equipment in or the gas out."

"Until now," she said defiantly and continued, "I was given the task by my company of making the situation work, of finding the solution. This is what I have accomplished."

The room became a little quieter as her stunned audience considered the implications.

"Our preliminary findings show that there are considerable reserves of both oil and gas."

"Yes, surely this is old news," the reporter interrupted, once again. She glared at him as she held her breath and the wicked smile rose as the glare faded.

She clicked a remote control and the projector flooded the screen with images. "Perhaps until today. This is some of the mobile equipment we have been using while we conducted feasibility studies. Our best estimates have been comfortably exceeded and we are confident that there are sizeable deposits locked in the valley folds. You are right," she now directed her laser pointer aggressively at the reporter who'd dared to interrupt her, "this is not much use without access. We have solved this problem by acquiring the land associated with the West Pennine surgery which will be closing under the direction of the Clinical Commissioning Authority and re-opening a little distance away in the centre of Horwich. This leaves us more than enough space to gain the access we need. Hundreds of jobs will be created. On this basis Carob Oil and Gas have applied for a drilling and fracking licence."

Another reporter raised his hand. "My information says that a bid has already gone in for the land as indicated on your map. I believe a bid for £180 million has gone in and been accepted. It isn't your company who've made that bid?"

"Well now, that would be a shame, if your reports are correct. It isn't our company that has tabled that bid." Dark eyes glared at the reporter but she could not quite hide the self-satisfied smile as it formed on her hungry expression.

"A shame, for whom? For you?"

She suppressed the laugh but she could not hide the enjoyment which ran through her entire body, its stance and in particular her expression.

"Oh, no, no, no." She held her lips together ostentatiously as if chastising a wayward child.

"A shame for the person who's spent £180 million."

"Why is that?" asked another reporter, just as she knew he must.

"Simply because," she paused as if summoning a fact that would be obvious even to a child, "they would have wasted their money."

"And why is that?" asked yet another reporter in the room that was now gripped by the words that came from her lips with their garish bright lipstick.

"The key, as one of you hinted at earlier, is access. I purchased the West Pennine surgery together with its car park some days ago. I am afraid that without access, access that can only be gained through this site, then their investment would be worthless. All the fracking rights in the world cannot overcome this obstacle, I am afraid." with fear being the last emotion to inhabit her cruel yet unconcerned expression.

She continued shaking her head as if disappointing a child, "One would simply not be able to get the rigs and the drilling equipment in without it. I'm afraid it would be a rather expensive flop," she looked at one of her acrylic, bright red nails as her features displayed a total lack of concern.

"The land is undoubtedly worth much more but without access..." The most uncomfortable of pauses followed as her words hung in the air and she now glared at them defiantly, hoping someone would argue with her. She then took up more of a whimsical air that was as entirely false as one of her nails.

"Buying such a thing without access, well it could ruin someone don't you think? This is why it's taken so long. Nobody had a clue what to do with it until I came along." She continued to glare but there was much more of a smug, self-satisfied overlay now.

The room became quiet, TV cameras rolled and some flashes went off: she met all of these without blinking.

The room murmured but then became deathly silent. It appeared that some consideration, was being given to the plight of the purchaser who had spent a lot of money on something that was worthless, at least without her bestowing mercy. Surely, such a thing was a rare visitor to her psyche.

She began speaking again, very slowly as if really having

to stretch her benevolence to its absolute maximum. "I suppose, in a bout of *absolute* generosity we'd be prepared to buy out such a person, the one who'd made such an ill-conceived and foolhardy purchase, shall we say for 1p in the pound."

The press pack, who waited eagerly for every word from her lips in the stunned and quiet room, now gasped collectively.

"So, you'll only offer one hundredth of their investment?" asked a reporter who clicked his recorder to make sure that he had missed nothing.

"Too generous do you think?" she offered without a hint of shame.

The room gasped again.

If such a thing were possible her expression followed her mood into darker hues.

"Perhaps this is the price that one pays for interfering in others' business; perhaps it will teach them a sharp lesson." Her voice now sped up and became more strident. She'd reached her point, all else was a preamble, "In any event the offer stands for 48 hours and then an offer of 0.1 p in the pound will be the only one remaining."

More flashes went off and more questions were murmured as hands were raised.

"But, but that's only £180,000 out of one hundred and eighty million?" The reporter, who still clung to his recorder, clarified.

"Yes, your maths are correct, quite correct."

Only one question impacted on her consciousness. She was growing tired of this group of nobodies.

"Surely, that would all but bankrupt such a person."

She now tittered like a schoolgirl, clearly enjoying her moment. The moment she'd crushed another opponent.

"Yes, I'm rather afraid it might. Perhaps they should have thought of that earlier."

She looked directly at one of the TV cameras as it zoomed in on her face, the laughter now being displaced totally for one of absolute confidence coupled to undiluted triumph. She couldn't wait to tell her lover.

"Meeting over, all. Game over, I believe. Thank you, all."

Flashes fired off again but Ms Makepeace stood and walked out of the room with her heavy yet confident steps. She had had enough. She'd done what she'd intended and the rest was just so much chaff. Victory tasted far too sweet to spend it with such wasters and those who were naïve enough to take her on. Now, everyone knew what she did to those who dared to even think of coming up against her.

So many watched the news feed. Although they were all shocked, and several were upset, at least they now understood. Their treatment at the hands of another finally made some sense and along with their learning came the satisfaction that often accompanies knowledge. It didn't sit easily that they had been duped in this way. The thoughts of the receptionists in particular were painful ones until they considered that others had fared worse and one or two had fared worst of all. Although it was far too late to change the reality of their catastrophe, Dr Binder finally understood. So many of the ex-staff realised too that they had been pawns in a much wider and crueller game. Susan simply stared at the TV screen as she realised just who had been in their midst all this time and what her real purpose had been. How could they have hoped to stand against such a person; how could anyone ever hope to take her on? They realised, to a woman, that they had lost a lot but at least one of their number had lost much more and, though it gave them no comfort to think of such a thing, they realised that they would perhaps be free to fight another day, unlike that person.

CHAPTER XIII

Woman Scorned

Amanda went back to the surgery. Notices had been put up directing patients to temporary medical services pending the imminent opening of Dr Rapace's surgery where they would all be invited to register.

As she went up to her room she noticed that Dr Rapace was in his room. She licked her lips in anticipation of a further torrid sexual encounter. Her recent success and absolute destruction of those who had the temerity to take her on always made her feel hungry for some flesh on flesh and she knew he would supply it.

She burst in to Dr Rapace's room, gripping his arms with more force than passion; more pain than stimulation. She almost ripped his jacket from him and clawed at his tie with the long nails.

He had been watching the morning news, broadcast live on TV. He realised he'd been used, as had all the others.

"Look, Mandy, not so rough."

"You didn't complain last time or the time before."

He pushed her away using a lot less force than she'd employed on him. He looked at her. His expression reflected the fact that something was not quite right as if suddenly a fit of conscience had befallen him.

"You told *me* you were going to open a school. You told me we needed to get old misery guts out so you could start your refurbishment. I didn't realise you were working all along for a *fracking* company." His emphasis on that word sounded even more like a swear word than it usually did.

"And, getting rid of Dr Binder didn't suit *your* purposes, I assume. It was okay for you to have your agenda but not for me, is that it?"

"I just feel a little upset about the deceit and the lies."

"And, of course, deceit and lies all fall on my shoulders. You are whiter than white in that regard. Is that what you tell your wife?"

"That's not the same."

"That's *exactly* the same. Okay, I lied to a few people; the ones you were planning to jettison as soon as you were able, I believe. Where has your sudden conscience come from?"

"I just feel as if I have been used." She laughed, yet another man with dual standards, judging a woman who dared to have plans of her own.

"Look here, Mandy, now that I am going to be principal of the largest surgery in the West Pennine moors, I don't think that our little affair is the right thing for me. I now have standards to uphold."

"And I don't fit in with those standards? So, you used me to pass the time until you were ready to move on?" Long talons moved quickly behind her back as she zipped up her skirt with finality, almost as if she were tightening a noose.

"This was a mutually beneficial diversion, Mandy."

Although she recognised the truth in his words, he'd missed something very important about the manager and he was about to gain an abject lesson as to exactly what this was. She was many things, but diversion wasn't one of them.

It was often quoted that revenge is a dish best served cold and this had appeared in several films. Much more apt, however, was that hell hath no fury like a woman scorned. Dr Rapace was about to be intimately and destructively acquainted with these little quotations.

Nobody dumped her, not until she was ready and even then nobody extracted himself or herself without paying a price that would ensure they would never forget their act of sheer folly. The irony was that she had just been about to jettison him, now that she had no further use for him; now that she had no further use for any of them. She had been about to humiliate him as soon as she'd got the clothes off his back. The performance, such as it was, that he could manage was a lot less than her other lovers had been capable of. He had been someone she'd used to break up the tedium and she had been planning on telling him exactly this just as she left. Now, however, she would put in motion something that was even sweeter and even more impactful.

How much those few, hasty, incautious words were about to cost him. No doubt he would forever regret having said them. This was no longer her concern.

She let him go and readjusted her skirt. "Very well then, I'll get the things I came for." The few words she spoke to him before she went up to her room left him with no indication as to what was about to befall him. He rubbed his neck wondering if new bruises were about to appear there and looked down at his shirt to see if it were blood-stained.

Amanda quickly found the things that she'd come back to the surgery for. Now, however, she sat at her desk crunching decisively on an apple as she waited until she heard his car start. She looked through her upstairs window as his large Audi, in gunmetal, began its ascent of the long dirt track back to the main road.

She then moved quickly. She placed the call as soon as he'd left. Her voice was calm, clear and deadly. The trick, as she knew only too well, was to speak first and deliver, without a pause, the words that would gain devastating momentum.

She dialled his home landline. The call was answered, but she had already begun speaking,

"Darling, where are you, I've been waiting for you, my sexy hot lips. I've a real aching for you tonight. I'm desperate, I need you now. I've been texting you my hot Tomcat, but there's no answer."

"Hello, who is this?"

"Is that 7418239?"

"Yes, it is. Who is this and who are you?"

"Oh, just a friend, who are you?" Was said with as much innocence as she could muster.

"I am Mrs Rapace."

"Oh sorry, I must have the wrong number after all, good day."

The phone was slammed down quickly, but the spark had already lit the fuse and this was now burning with an unquenchable ferocity.

Once again, the long index finger had destroyed another as it danced over the keypad numbers. One short call was all that was required to ensure that the man who'd dared to cross her paid the price, with compounded interest, for his fatal transgression. The smile, one of undiluted revenge, was forming on her face even before she put the phone down. She knew all too well that a few well chosen and directed words were all that was required to obliterate a man and his marriage, such as it was. Few crossed Amanda Makepeace and lived to tell the tale. Come to think of it even from her schooldays none had dared to cross her or even think they could get the better of her.

Dr Rapace's marriage was over long before he got home. In point of fact, fifteen years of marriage was terminated in almost as many seconds.

Muriel Rapace knew that all she'd have to do to confirm her new-found discovery would be to check his mobile phone. However, the delay and uncertainty this entailed was no longer required: for she was now in no mood for delay. Furthermore, she was now certain. In truth, she'd had suspicions for some time. He'd been working late for so many nights; many more nights than she thought were necessary to secure his future at the new surgery. There had also been unusual marks on his body, round his neck and torso. She'd also noticed blood on his shirts and underclothes. How stupid she'd been. In that moment, the most painful and abrupt of realisations came to her; she knew that very little work had been going on.

She'd also wondered how he could scheme and plot against his former friend and former partner. Admittedly, Neil Binder had let things get away from him, but he in no way deserved the fate that her husband and that woman at the surgery had selected for him. This was especially so since the dreadful accident that had claimed his family. It had always sat uneasily upon her and now she realised that she could rid herself of so much baggage that she no longer needed.

As Fergus Rapace cheerily entered through the front door, he saw the pile of clothes that had been chaotically tossed on the circular rug that lay in the middle of their extensive hall. The large rug was almost covered by the substantial quantity. Initially, he thought that his wife must be having a clear-out of some of her own clothes but then he recognised that the material was, in fact, all his handmade wool and cashmere suits that had been shredded in a frenzy of rage. And right on the top were remnants of his equally precious, hand-made silk ties that had received similar treatment.

Far from being upset or angry, his wife was now cool enough for him to know that she'd passed into a much more deliberative frame of mind and this did not bode well. For her calmness indicated that a judgement had been made, with no possibility of appeal, and a sentence had been passed but was only yet to be served. Only then did he notice the large suitcase.

Her voice was calm and clear. "Don't' say anything, you'll just be wasting your breath. I'll be claiming half the house, half your savings and, of course, half your pension. Please find what you can of your personal effects and leave the key on the table before you leave; you may take the suitcase. All other negotiations will henceforth be through my solicitor."

His sentence began, "Muriel, can we talk about..." Only the shaking of her head indicated the futility of further words on his part. She turned and went upstairs. She didn't glance back. Such a move was for those who were in some way unsure, or undecided, or not ready to commit to final irrevocable acts and she was none of these things.

He did as he was asked; it only took him a few minutes to find a few basic effects that her dressmaker's shears had not encountered. He closed the door behind him and no further words were spoken.

Quite apart from the end of his marriage, he realised that he'd lost far more. The loans that he'd taken out to finance the new surgery were based on financial wherewithal that he no longer controlled.

He had no doubt that his wife would bring about her threat to claim half his assets and the divorce judge would ensure that this was carried out. His loans, as well as his financial position, had in that moment passed from a healthy glow to the critical list. His plans were as ashes at his feet. Estate agents loved a fire sale and with his wife baying for half of the entire estate – she would ensure that things were carried out at her convenience and on her terms. He knew that any attempt to contest the proceedings that would now engulf him would be met by the finest legal counsel that half of his money could buy. Moreover, she was from a wealthy family. They would make sure she received every assistance.

He was about to jump back into his expensive Audi but then he realised that it had been a present to him from her parents. He had a feeling that even this had now passed into the realm of what was to be negotiated rather than what was his. He called a taxi as he stood on what had once been his porch.

He shivered against the cold of the night made so much worse by the sight of his wool and cashmere overcoat in shreds on what looked like a pyre, yet to be lit, of his entire wardrobe. The only things he now had of which he was certain were contained in a suitcase that had been set down next to him and didn't of itself weigh very much.

On the outskirts of Horwich in a rented flat above a newsagent, Petunia stared through the window deep in thought. The tall man had popped out to get himself a takeaway. Petunia said that she wasn't hungry; sickness had totally destroyed her appetite.

As the final act in the disaster in evolution enveloped the young woman, her thoughts now were only for others. She considered all those that she might have been able to help, to support and save. She had run out of resources now to enable her to help any of them. It seemed that her final act was simply whether she could save herself, her husband and her aunt – the one she'd promised to look after forever. Notwithstanding all of this, there remained one more promise that she knew she had to keep. She was determined to enact it now.

Ultimately, what saved her that day were the thoughts that she held for the little old lady and the need to protect her from the chaos that was about to be unleashed in her quiet and uneventful life. She knew that she could not and would not sell those rights so expensively acquired without first consulting with the person that it would affect the most.

She choked back the tears. These, she had promised herself, would be the last. Once they were swept from the pretty face, then there would be no more.

The following morning Petunia placed a Skype call to Mr Bloor. He looked downcast and sad, even worse than did Petunia who'd passed through what she would refer to as her phase of self-pity and was now at least in a more practical frame of mind.

"I am so sorry, my dear, to hear of your reversal at the hands of that woman. One of my colleagues has dealings with Carob Oil and he tells me that they are all a nasty, greedy bunch who would sell their own grandmothers for two and six."

She smiled as he suddenly blushed; even his grey eyebrows seemed to take on a pinkish hue. It certainly wasn't like Archibald Bloor to dismiss anyone so unfavourably.

"I am afraid that the transfer has completely drained your account. We even had to include some interest payments that you are technically due at the end of the month. I am sure you realise the highly irregular nature of such artifice."

"Yes, yes of course, Mr Bloor, and I thank you for doing that for me. I would never want you to endanger your own position over me."

Now the elderly man smiled, "I have been here so long, my dear, that I think any attempt to remove me would cause even these hallowed walls to crumble and fall."

She smiled in return. "I was wondering what options are open to me?"

"Of course, we would be happy to extend you a facility, if you so wish. You have always indicated to me, however, that you would never wish to take on such a thing."

"Yes, that is correct, Mr Bloor."

"It remains then, for me to suggest that you take up that dreadful woman's offer of 1p in the pound," his expression became angry as he said the words and reminded himself of the methods of Ms Makepeace. "You will have just shy of two million pounds and this will allow you to retain your house in Vancouver as well as at least keep you solvent."

"Trouble is with this I would have to release the land to Carob Oil and Ms Makepeace."

He coughed a little awkwardly and suddenly blushed again, "If I may venture, my dear. You have done your best. Perhaps it is time to think of yourself. Save yourself, and let us not forget about your aunt who depends upon you?"

"That is very true, Mr Bloor, thank you for your wise counsel." She nodded but in point of fact, although the banker always gave her options, he very rarely ventured an opinion. Perhaps his opinions were vested in his grave visage that continued to look back at her sorrowfully.

"So, am I correct in thinking that without Ms Makepeace's *kind* offer," they both shuddered a little as she ran through the word, "that I have no funds whatsoever?"

"Well, my dear, what have you in mind?"

"I was hoping to move a little old lady. Her house would be in the path of the new development. I cannot under any circumstances let them go ahead until, and unless, she is protected. I was also hoping to pay someone's mortgage off."

"You would do such a thing for others, and yet put yourself in a financially fragile state in order to do so. May I enquire how much there is outstanding on the mortgage in question?"

"I have told you, Archibald, that this money is of no use to me; it represents only how much I can do for others. Oh, and as regards the mortgage it is £25,000 in total."

He smiled, from anyone but this wonderful young woman such words would appear as false and artificial. How he wished he were a younger man.

"Very well then, I suspect you will be able to do one of these things but, sadly not both. If you'd permit me, however, to make a suggestion to you. I have just had a meeting with Peter Perkins, the young man whose name I am sure you will recognise. Your instinct about him, and the forgiveness you showed him, were not misplaced. He has become one of my most diligent and capable employees and he is very keen to assist you now. If I might suggest also that this is very dear to his heart and I would strongly urge you to give this your most serious consideration."

"Archibald, that is so kind of you and Mr Perkins. I wonder then if we might proceed as follows?"

She outlined her intended strategy to him and he could only nod and think all over again how wonderful this young woman was and how lucky he had been to receive her the day she walked into his offices.

"Very well, my dear, that sounds eminently suitable. It is a pleasure to speak with you and many thanks for contacting me and for informing me of your plans. I do wish you every good fortune, my dear, and I am so sorry to see that things have turned against you. I am sure that your resilient nature will shine through, however, these dark days."

"Always, always, thank you so much Archibald. And thank you for your kind thoughts."

That same day in one of the side streets that led away from the village centre in Horwich, and not two miles away from the surgery that had been closed, a young woman tapped on a UPVC door as she perched uncertainly on the narrow step. She looked up at the leaden sky and bent a little against the wind that, even here, swept in from the moors. The portly gentleman who opened the door stood there disinterestedly. His string vest and shorts were stretched unhappily by his expanding paunch which was made even more noticeable by his lack of height.

The young, untidy woman with an unruly fringe waited patiently on the step, not having been invited in. The tubby gentleman, she reasoned, was the father of the person she was visiting. She asked him if Susan was at home.

He looked her up and down. He saw the worn blouse, the untidy slacks that seemed a little too long for her even though she was a fair height; he estimated at five foot eight. Such things were an irrelevance to him; he had more important things to worry about.

One thing he did notice, however, was the magnificent watch on her left wrist. Years before he'd been a watch salesman in a local branch of a nationwide chain of jewellers' shops. Hard times had set in; the local shop had been closed in favour of larger, more prestigious branches at the Trafford Centre and Liverpool One. His eyes widened as he locked on to it. There was nothing low-rent about that watch which he recognised immediately as a high-end item that sat comfortably around the girl's wrist. The even more puzzling thing – for he'd made a study of such watches and the people who purchased them – was that despite her untidiness and her overall appearance the watch itself seemed in no way out of place. If he wasn't mistaken, and he wasn't mistaken, it was a Cartier Santos.

This, sadly, drew him back to a time now long gone and he was no longer interested in such irrelevancies. He had much more pressing matters to attend to, such as how they were going to cope now that his daughter had, somehow, lost her job.

He stared just for a moment longer before dismissing the image of the young woman, and her watch. This was all part of a previous life when he had work, more than a little pride and yes; he'd been good at his job. He shook his head as if now physically clicking himself back to his current life; one in which he believed he had no worth and no value, not even to himself, let alone to others. He raised his head and turned it so that he could call out, " It's for you, Sue," in his booming voice that shook the front window.

With this he moved away with no further words being spoken. He offered only silence and his back to the woman who waited now a little nervously on the front step in the gathering dullness of yet another bleak day. She shrugged off the unedifying sight of his large bottom barely covered by his drooping shorts. Mercifully, the images and his back receded into the dark confines of the little house with each step he took. Susan appeared moments later, coming through the glass-panelled door that separated the front room from the back room and kitchen as she did so.

"Didn't think I'd see you again. I saw the telly. I am sorry she defeated you. I'm sorry you lost going up against her."

"It happens," Petunia acknowledged as embarrassment rose on her otherwise bright features.

"I might have known she was too crafty, too strong. Nobody could have beaten her. I should have guessed she was after something; something really important, really valuable. And she was!"

"Look, I am sorry you lost your job over me. I was hoping I could have done more…"

The painful pause opened as she looked down.

"Don't worry about it, Petunia. I just had a hunch you could take her on and beat her. My hunch was wrong. No crime, no foul. I'll get another job. There's a new supermarket opening in town. They've had two hundred applications for thirty jobs, but, hey, it's a start isn't it? They might just fish my application out, even without a reference from Ms Makepeace."

"It said on the news that things had gone badly for you. They say she's got you by the throat and will squeeze till you hand over that land. They all say you are ruined. I'm sorry if that's the case."

"Oh, don't you worry about me. I'll live to fight another day. Look, Susan, I know this isn't much but I wanted to give you this. I hope it will tide you over until you find work."

Susan looked at the cheque made out to her in respect of a thousand pounds. She raised her left eyebrow briefly.

"Wow, that's generous and I thank you, most sincerely, but I don't want your money or your charity. I did what I did because I thought it was the right thing. I would have lost my job anyway as soon as the surgery closed. It ain't your fault and I ain't your responsibility. We are fine; you don't owe me a nickel. My dad wasn't too happy but he's seen that the surgery is closed anyway. He knew what a tricky customer Ms Makepeace was and he'd heard about all those she'd got rid of. I was simply one of the latest in a long chain." She looked pink with embarrassment and her words had run out; there was nothing else to be said. With this Susan hugged Petunia, coming down from the top step in order to do so. She returned the cheque to her visitor. Just before she turned to go back into the depths of the house she raised another eyebrow to ask, "So, what you going to do now? Now it's all over for you?"

"As I said to Dr Binder, I'm going to get my hair cut."

"Yes, good move, could do with a trim if not a good shearing! Goodbye Petunia, and thanks for calling. Don't you worry about me, I'll be fine and we'll be fine. That's if my mum doesn't kill him for being under her feet all day!"

With this, Susan turned and went back into the house. Just before the front door closed Petunia heard the sound of loud and violent shouting coming from within.

CHAPTER XIV

Redemption

A little later the same day at a not dissimilar house, albeit one that was in a much better state of repair, not a mile away, a tall young man stood on the top step having tapped on the front door.

Emma Sparkle was just putting her coat on when the knock came on the entrance to her little terraced house in Horwich. She knew who it was before she opened her front door. She'd had her fair share of people who knocked just like that. The other point was that they'd been writing to her a lot of late. She knew without opening any of those letters what they contained and now, no doubt, someone had been sent to do their bidding and carry out their threats.

Opening the door, she looked knowingly at the tall, thin, young man wearing a grey suit, white shirt and blue tie. Standing on the step of the small but beautiful stone-built cottage made him appear even taller.

She looked the handsome man up and down. "I know who you are."

He looked surprised at this, but before he could speak, she continued, "Bit late, though."

He looked with even more surprise

"You do? And I am?" he queried.

"I'm on my way to the bus stop, laddie. Been offered a cleaning job at the new surgery, in town. Still, got half an hour if you need me to sign summat?"

"You have? And I do, if you don't mind?"

"Yes, won't save me, though. I know, I owe too much."

"It won't? And you do?"

"Yes, yes I can spot you suits a mile off. Don't you worry, I know why you are here."

"You do?"

"Course I do. I might be old to a young stripling like you, but my brain ain't addled, as yet anyhow. Unless of course you ain't there and I'm talkin' to myself." She laughed at both her own levity in difficult circumstances and the expression on his face. "I even know what your gonna say. nothing personal, just doin' your job. You've come from the bank."

She sensed more puzzlement rising on his face.

"I have. But, how did you know that?"

"I told you. I might be poor but I ain't daft. You suits; can spot you a mile away. Not being offensive, like. I've had so many of you types standing just there on my little doorstep. Don't take exception n'all, but you all look the same to me. Clean shaven, pressed suit, fresh-faced youngsters, like you. Mind you, they all had briefcases. They've been threatening for ages. Knew they'd bang on the door one day and 'ere you are, eh laddo. " She looked down at the case perched on the step. "Ay yes, just like that one." She laughed again.

"Really?"

"You'd better come in then laddie, but I ain't got much time. Not if I'm gonna get this job or I'll be in even greater debt. "

She sensed still more surprise queuing on his features.

"I am, here to do my job, I mean."

"You are from the bank, right? And you've come about the house?"

"I am, and I have. But how did you know?"

"Told yer, been expectin yer like. You've come to fore… fore…, call in the mortgage and throw me out on the street?"

The tall young man had followed her into the front room but remained standing now clutching his black case. He laughed but then he paused. He had been wrong-footed by the conversation on the doorstep. He knew that Petunia would have done things differently. Firstly she'd have paused, then she'd have smiled, then kindness itself would have flowed seamlessly, with every thought, every word and action. Trouble was, he was having a great deal of difficulty getting a word in edgewise, with this animated older lady.

"It's nothing to laugh about. I know, I know, you don't need to tell me. I've had plenty of warning. Good job my sister will put me up. I know you are simply the messenger, that's what you all say. Some big wig in the bank; someone I've never met and don't even know me, never set foot in Horwich, has drawn a red line, or whatever they do, through my file and told you to come here and turf me out of my home. I know they've been patient; much more than I expected since I fell behind with the payments, but I just couldn't raise that sort of money with my cleaning jobs, not since my Bill died that is."

She went on in this way for some time further. Her talk was good-natured enough and without bitterness or malice as she had clearly become resigned to her fate. Indeed it was only when she looked at her wristwatch that she realised she was going to have to hurry if she was going to catch the bus into town. Her words faded quickly, but with no other indication that she had run out of words and was about to stop. The young man decided he had better simply wait until the rush of speech had calmed a little. When he saw her look at her watch he knew now might be a good opportunity.

"Mrs Sparkle, I am a banker, you are correct, and I have come about your house, you are correct in that, too. I am not here, however, to turn you out of your lovely home." He looked round the bijou parlour, sipping the tea that she'd assembled very quickly and pushed in front of him whilst she somehow maintained a steady flow of words. The case was now on his knee, there was so little space for him to put it down, and the teacup and saucer balanced precariously on it as his long legs projected forwards as he perched on the small sofa. He saw speech forming on her lips again and knew he'd have to keep talking. His failure to continue before she started talking again could only mean a significant delay and, although the young man was in no particular hurry, he realised that her need to catch her bus was of importance to her. His speech sped up.

"I work for a large bank in the centre of Manchester and we manage funds for very wealthy clients. As part of this work we undertake to provide assistance to those who might need a bit of a helping hand. People of sound character, like yourself, who have always tried to do the right thing and have, nevertheless, suffered. I am here…" he saw her mouth moving again as she was about to launch more questions. He knew that pausing would be unwise and he therefore did his best to speed his speech up even more and compensated for any loss of clarity by raising his voice as much as politeness would allow. "I am here to provide you with some assistance. Financial assistance and there are no strings attached. I am here to offer you £25,000 immediately. I have the cheque here and it's been made out in your name." Finally he paused, hoping that he'd conveyed his meaning and done so in a way in which Petunia would have done had she been here, albeit at a much slower and more measured pace.

"But I cannot afford that sort of money, that's why I have to leave. I understand that," she said looking intently at her visitor as if he had not quite understood things. "You don't have to trick me, I can be out of the house in the next day or two."

Peter Perkins smiled. "Mrs Sparkle, I can assure you that this money is yours." He reached into his case and extracted a piece of paper containing more information, which he waved in front of her. "One of our wealthy clients has provided this money, for your use and there are no strings attached. You can use this sum of money to settle your debts once and for all."

"But, but, I can't afford it, that's why I am going."

The young man smiled again and knew that further reassurance was needed. He reached out somewhat awkwardly but his long arms were able to accomplish the task. He held her hand gently. "Worry not, this house is now yours, forever."

Mrs Sparkle had clearly discovered the secret of perpetual motion for her lips continued to move, although her speech had petered out.

As he handed over the cheque she looked at it like a wish that had been made on an angel's wing on a sunny afternoon; one that was about to disappear. She remained more startled than anything and this was a good thing as it allowed him to continue at a more measured pace.

He nodded, "It's all yours and just yours, I can assure you. You may telephone my bank if you wish. I can promise you, however, that I am here to help you not trick you."

"But who? Who has done this for me, I don't know anyone?"

"Well, you must know someone, because they have put your name forward."

"But who's paid this money?"

Peter Perkins repeated, "A kind benefactor has made this sum available to a worthy cause and it was determined that you were that worthy cause."

"But who? Who would do that for me?"

"We may never know, in truth, Mrs Sparkle, but a wealthy benefactor has left instructions," he lied, for the third time in that sentence, for he, Peter Perkins, knew precisely who the person was who'd provided the money.

He also knew that he could never reveal that at a desperate hour, now some time ago, he'd been given a chance just like the one he was making available to the ageing cleaner; he was now doing something that he always promised himself he would do, repay that favour to another, as soon as he was able. He was simply making good on that promise given all those months ago.

From being unable to stop talking, Emma found that absolute speechlessness now descended on her.

He folded her hand gently over the cheque hoping that this too would provide some further reassurance despite the state of numbed shock that rose on her face in that moment.

For some minutes she looked at the cheque staring at it to see if it were really a hoax or a nasty joke of some kind. Yet, it looked real; it had that heavy glossy paper and the swirly watermarks, barcodes and funny numbers along the bottom. More importantly, it was swirled over by a lovely flowing signature that carried the simple message 'pay Emma Sparkle twenty five thousand pounds.'

He sensed her thoughts. "I can tell you that it is quite genuine. Furthermore, I can also tell you that if you present it to a bank tomorrow it will be paid in to your account immediately and without question. If you prefer, and are able to travel into Manchester, if you present it at my bank the notes will be handed over to you subject only to your providing proof as to who you are."

He smiled filially at her as he rose to go. He insisted on shaking her hand; congratulating her on her deliverance. With almost explosive speed, she leapt forwards to hug him as she danced round the front room of the stone-built cottage that was now hers. She looked at her watch. "Oh, my goodness, my bus! I'll miss it, and my new job."

"Well, Mrs Sparkle, we can't have you missing a job opportunity. If you'd permit me, I'd be happy to give you a lift to wherever you need to be."

She stared at this bright young man and couldn't help but reach up to grab him, as best her height permitted, round the neck in order to hug and kiss him.

Peter straightened his tie, his cheek was wet with the slobbery kiss she'd imparted. He pulled himself up to his full height despite the low ceilings and led her out to his car which was parked just down the main road.

He walked with much delight being shown on his face though nothing like as much of the same emotion now registered on hers as she gazed at the cheque like a magic spell that had appeared from another dimension. She tucked the cheque into her purse as they walked. He made easy strides on his long legs as she almost skipped with delight while she kept up with him with much smaller ones.

Peter Perkins looked up at the grey clouds that parted just for an instant, allowing a sliver of pure sunshine to illuminate for a second or two the pavement along which they now walked. Even the penetrating wind seemed to withdraw compliantly from the scene as they went forwards. Much more than this, however, he knew that the person who'd given him his break, when his job was threatened and his wife had been heavily pregnant, would smile with a resonance that matched his.

A little later the same day, Petunia was sitting in the stylist's chair as he, once again, made an attempt to tame what many thought could not be tamed. His scissors chattered quickly and expertly as her wonderful tresses were ordered and brought into a stunning focus. In due course, the bright blue eyes were liberated and their illimitable intensity shone like a glowing beam as she smiled back at all those who couldn't help but look at her again and again. As the hairdresser paused Petunia noted that a message had come through on her iPhone. She was desperate to open the message and it was all she could do to patiently wait until the stylist went to get her a cup of coffee so that she could view it.

'Thank you so much for helping me and my wife all those months ago. When things were at a low ebb you placed trust, and showed confidence, in me. I hope my actions today have shown how sincere I am in my gratitude and desire to help another in this way, just when she needed a little kindness.' Petunia smiled, a little tear presented in the corner of her eye, just as the stylist returned with her cup of coffee and to finish his work.

The off-white mini waited for her as she came out of the hairdresser's.

"That's more like it," he said enthusiastically, "back to your fabulous self."

She smiled but didn't feel remotely fabulous. Moreover she knew that she had the more difficult of the two calls she'd planned for that day to make and even the first had not gone particularly well.

"Well, here we go, on to Mrs Spencer's house."

The mini turned off the main road just before the lay by and bus stop. They drove down the long lane and approached the lonely house just as the murky day was passing into night. For once, the wind had subsided and the chill was nowhere near as noticeable. A brilliant moon rose in the night sky as he parked the car a little way from the house and she took a deep breath as she vacated the Mini.

CHAPTER XV

Ace

Petunia stood on Mrs Spencer's porch as Bobby the ginger tom glared at her suspiciously. This time, however, a glint of familiarity meant that he stood his ground as she approached. He meowed just a little and as she looked down at him he started moving towards her. A gust of wind unsettled him and he decided to stay where he was. The only discomfort he displayed was some shuffling from the large and furry paws as she tapped quietly on the door. Bobby glanced up but then looked away with a disdainful air. He padded along the wooden veranda and two subservient cats moved away as he approached.

Matilda responded to the quiet tap with an animated push on the door as if she were eager to see who was there. Petunia had forgotten that the door opened outwards and was nearly swept off the top step as the door came towards her with almost more speed than surprise would allow.

Matilda paused before her face lit up as she recognised the young woman who was standing there.

"Oh, hello. My what a nice surprise! I wasn't expecting to see *you* today," lied the old lady.

"And, if I may say, looking absolutely gorgeous! What a pretty thing you are. Back to your old self."

"Pardon?"

"Oh, I was thinking out loud. I was wondering if you were feeling better after the shock of the surgery closing?"

She swung the door open even further and stood back a little as she invited the former receptionist into the dark hallway that retained a slight cat-centred odour.

Matilda chattered away nervously she could tell that Petunia had been crying.

"So, to what do I owe this wonderful, unexpected visit? Have I left a prescription at the surgery?" she lied twice in as many false questions.

Petunia smiled weakly, but at least the tears had been banished. Her face, however, continued to display the deathly pallor that had haunted it for the past few days.

"Please forgive me, Mrs Spencer, but something terrible has happened. It took me a while to figure out what's going on and now it looks as if it might be too late."

"Oh my goodness, that sounds serious. You'd better sit down," she offered with more seriousness than she could feel inside.

"Can I ask you, are you still experiencing the noise at night?"

"Well, it's been quiet for the past few nights, just when Dr Binder referred me to the ear people at the hospital. Thank you for asking but is that why you look so worried?"

"In a way, yes. The moorland down the valley is rich in shale gas and probably oil."

"Oh, they've always known that," confirmed the older lady dismissively, "they can't get to it, you see. There have been so many schemes but all have failed. They have tried and tried but never worked out a way to get to it. Please don't worry about that; at least not on my account."

"Well, I'm afraid now they think they can. That's why it's now worth so much. Dr Binder's surgery is the key. Once that has been acquired then they can use the surgery and its car park as a base. That base can then be used for access. With the equipment in place then they can extract the gas and transport it all out. I realised, far too late, that this is why the manager was here all along. She was just waiting for the surveys to confirm that the land is very valuable with rich stocks of oil and gas. Then she ran the surgery down and managed to persuade Dr Binder to sell it to her under the pretext of opening a school for disadvantaged children."

The older lady looked thoughtful for a moment and then shook her head. "You know, I never did like her. I always wondered what business she had there. She ran that place into the ground. So many good staff were pushed out. I can see why now."

"Yes, I didn't realise just what she was up to until it was too late. It's not too late to stop her, but I wanted to talk with you first."

"This sounds very important and it is good of you to consider an old girl like me."

"No, not at all. The noise you hear at night is the plant and machinery being brought onto the site. Carob Oil and Gas is a large exploration company. They seek out new supplies. The area is so sensitive that they wanted to be sure before they put a bid in and also wanted to get the land as cheaply as possible. They tried to hide it by only working at night. They didn't want anyone to know they were there and what they were doing."

"So, what part do you play in all this?"

"I was sent a letter from someone; someone who remains anonymous. They asked me to help. I think they were concerned for Dr Binder and for the surgery. Of course, I can see why now. In truth though, it's a bigger game than just poor Dr Binder. He, as well as his surgery, is just a pawn in a far bigger game. I thought I could help, that is why I tried to intervene, but I suspect I can do very little now. It's moved away from me."

"That is so good of you, to try to help, but you say the land is worth a lot of money? Forgive me, but a young woman like you..." the older lady let the words trail off as she had difficulty defining precisely what she meant and let the silence work for her instead.

"Well, that's a side issue. What I really came to tell you and to ask you is this. If the oil company get hold of that land, now that they own the surgery they will start full-scale oil and gas extraction. Your quiet home, here, will be the centre of operations. They will flatten the surgery and put up cabins for the men to work out of and heavy plant and lorries will drive past your house. The noise will be even worse and your cats will be terrified. Things may quieten down at night but I am not sure it will be right for you or your cats."

"Oh, don't you worry about me or my cats."

"But, Mrs Spencer, I am not sure you realise what the scale of operations will be like. I can still block them even though they have gained control of the surgery."

Mrs Spencer still did not realise the danger that she and her feline friends were in. At the most crucial point she seemed to wander off on a tangent.

"Ooh, did you hear about poor Dr Rapace. His wife's thrown him out. They say he's ruined. He'll never be able to afford that new surgery now. Couldn't have happened to a nicer chap." The older lady smiled mischievously, causing the younger to pause. More importantly Mrs Spencer still didn't seem to realise the seriousness of the situation and seemed altogether too jovial.

"Yes, I agree about Dr Rapace. Maybe he has his comeuppance but surely that is terrible news for the patients who were hoping to register there."

"Well, I reckon it will go for a song now."

Petunia paused. Mrs Spencer had taken on a whole new appearance and seemed much more animated than at any of their previous meetings. One thing was for sure; scatty old lady she was not. Petunia then began some mental calculations to see if she still had the financial wherewithal to purchase the surgery from Dr Rapace.

The older lady seemed to sense her thoughts just as the disappointment of realising that her financial penury meant she would be lucky to keep her house in Vancouver visited Petunia's features.

"Anyway, Mrs Spencer, I am here to warn you but also to reassure you. I think I can block their plans completely."

"But you say Dr Binder has sold the surgery to the manager, so surely it's out of your hands now isn't it? How can you block them?"

"Well, I've bid for the drilling rights - the rights to start the fracking. Technically although they have the surgery, I own the actual land that contains the oil and gas."

Mrs Spencer now stared at Petunia.

"You, you bought that land! My goodness it must have cost a fortune. And you did all this to help me and others. But if they own the surgery, which you tell me is the key to the whole thing; surely it will ruin you?"

"Well, it's not about the money; it's about helping others. It's about doing what I came to do. What I tried to do anyway." Petunia's voice trailed off.

"And it's ruined you! A young woman like you, with your life ahead of you and you want to save others."

"I should have known that the surgery was the key. I was outwitted, outsmarted."

"Just how could you have known that? Besides, I would say you were out-spited by someone who is used to playing a dirty game that perhaps your world has rarely seen."

"Others warned me of my folly. Somehow, I think I should have seen through it all."

The older lady smiled. "You know, Petunia, nobody is perfect and I suspect you did your best."

"I'm afraid it wasn't quite good enough."

"Well that's as maybe. We shall see. So why are you telling me all this?"

"Well, I can offer you two options. I can move you away from here, you and all your cats, somewhere away from all this. Or, I can block their plans by refusing to release the land that they want so badly. Their whole reason for being here in the first place."

"But, but why should I move when I am happy here?"

"Oh Mrs Spencer, you don't have to move, I promise. I can and I will block them if that's what you want."

"Oh, no. You can't do that for me. It says on the telly they've offered you a pittance for the land, anyway." Petunia stared just for a moment, obviously the elderly lady was more up with events than she'd previously hinted at, "It will ruin you and stop all the good work something tells me you have only just got started with. Don't you worry about me and my cats; we'll be fine here."

"Well, the surgery will be the centre of operations. They will level it and then use the land and the car park to bring in heavy equipment, drilling rigs, storage tanks. All that heavy plant will come down here." Petunia's voice trailed off again, even this news couldn't wipe away the curious little smile that the older lady's face still held.

"Ah yes, I believe it will."

"That noise you were experiencing in your head at night was just some of the equipment being brought in. When it starts up in earnest then I am afraid it will be even worse."

"Oh, I could do with a bit of excitement."

Petunia knew in that moment that Matilda had not quite grasped what was about to be unleashed upon her and her cats. She desperately tried to reframe the context, something that would focus the cat lover's thoughts.

"But what about you and your cats?"

"Oh, I think they'll be fine. Someone will save me and them, I think," she offered with a newly-resident glint in her eye, one that Petunia had not seen before

"Well, look that's why I am here. I can save you."

"You can?"

"Well, as I said, I can either block it by refusing to sell the rights or I can move you, whichever you would prefer."

"You, you'd do all that for me? But just how could you manage that? Forgive me but this sounds all rather expensive. Surely it would be better to take their offer, no?"

"Well, perhaps let me worry about that."

"But, but I'm guessing that that would cost a whole lot of money and, I suspect, has already cost you a considerable amount. Forgive me, but where has a young woman like you got all that money from?"

"Oh, that's a long story, but look, if you want to stay here I can block their plans. I don't have to sell to them or anyone for that matter and you can live here in peace." Petunia desperately tried to further their conversation but the old lady kept coming back to the money, while the young woman just wanted to do right by her.

"Well, Petunia, that really sounds like big money now and it sounds as if you'll be putting that up personally?"

"Well let's not worry about that. Money doesn't mean much if one doesn't do the right thing."

The old lady now laughed, the glow now firmly established in the pale grey eyes.

"One more person to save, eh?"

"Pardon?"

She laughed again. "You heard me, and I said, one more person to save?"

The two women now stared at each other as if the unexpected nature of the conversation had stalled its progress. Petunia in particular was stunned, hearing words she hadn't expected to hear. There was much more to come. All was not as it seemed. Furthermore, the older lady had clearly seen the news programme and had also understood its implications long before Petunia had arrived. Matilda, it was now clear, had taken on very different characteristics from the, at all times nice, but slightly scatty, elderly lady that Petunia had encountered only a few weeks before. Her words sped up, she was in a hurry, bonded to an enthusiasm that would have belied her age had it not been for the glint in her eye that was now unmissable.

Suddenly, the older lady sprang to her feet with a rapidity of movement that stunned Petunia even more.

"Come with me, my dear," she held out a thin, bony hand on the extremity of an even thinner and more bony arm.

She led the receptionist back to the hall. A spring had appeared in her step as she bounded forward, one that she seemed barely able to contain. She approached the front room, the door to which she'd closed hurriedly a few days before, which she now entered with something of a flourish. She motioned for Petunia to follow her inside just as she switched on the light. A rather dull bulb provided illumination but nothing could have prepared the young woman for what lay within. Petunia saw immediately that the walls in the whole room were lined with hundreds of newspaper cuttings, magazine articles and photographs. All were dedicated to just one person.

There was that speech again, faster than Petunia had remembered and, once again, with that business-like edge. "I'm sure you can see that I've been collecting these for quite some time. In point of fact, ever since I first heard about the young woman who features in all of these articles." She swept her arms around the room like a magician presenting her latest, seemingly impossible trick to a stunned audience. Petunia was rendered speechless by what she saw.

"Of the thousands of cuttings and articles, this one is my favourite." She pulled a letter that had been placed in a clear plastic folder off the wall. Petunia recognised the handwriting immediately. She gasped as she realised exactly where the letter had come from. Tears would have re-established themselves at this point had shock and surprise not appeared as the primary emotions now in charge of her consciousness.

"All these people, every single one, I've lost count of just how many there are. These are just the ones I know about, I suspect there will be hundreds more and you, my girl, saved each and every one of them. It's high time someone repaid the favour and saved you for once."

Petunia was still unable to speak.

Clinging to the letter Matilda had given her she glanced repeatedly from the letter to the adorned walls to the little old lady who had continued to take on many attributes other than those of a frail, old cat lady. At this point, a kind smile replaced the energy written to the older woman's face.

She nodded towards the letter. "He gave me that letter when I visited him." Her smile showing hints of both pride and excitement.

"You visited Ronald Rainger?"

"Yes I did," Matilda offered simply with a hint of fascination and triumph now added to the excitement on her visage.

"The bit I like the best is here." She pointed at the letter, a piece of paper that she obviously knew intimately, having read it so many times. She quoted then without having to look at it. "'You can return home and live there for as long as time will allow', how wonderful! I cannot tell you how many times I've read that little bit. Your words, I believe, my dear – *you* wrote that. It was just another in a long, long list of promises that you kept. No ifs or buts, you just got on and did it and, if I might add, ever so quietly so that, or so you hoped, nobody would ever notice – apart from those countless numbers of people that you have helped, of course." It was the older lady's turn to pause whilst the younger caught up.

She detected that the young receptionist was still a little overawed. "Well, I noticed and that's why I decided to write to you. I thought that if anyone could help him, Dr Binder, and help us, it was you. I'm so sorry that I put you in so much danger. I was so desperate to meet you after reading so much about you. I didn't realise just what was involved. It took me so long to figure it all out and it was only when I saw Missolini, 'cruel manager' on TV that it finally clicked for me."

"So it was you who wrote to me. Petunia pulled a letter out of her back pocket. I was wondering who it could possibly have been. I thought it must be one of the receptionists who'd been fired."

"No, my dear. Can you forgive me, I do hope I've not ruined you?"

"Please don't worry, as I said to you it doesn't mean much if you can't stand up and do the right thing. I knew it would all end one day. I've had a good run and I've been able to help a lot of people. Perhaps it is my time, time to move on and I should, perhaps, get a proper job." Petunia was disappointed and deeply so, and yet there was no bitterness in her expression, or her heart. Mrs Spencer had meant well and could not have anticipated the resulting turn of events.

However, not all had been said and the older lady made good on that in that instant.

"That's as may be but not today, your run isn't over yet and, in point of fact, I think it's only just beginning. You *have* a proper job and you have done so much. You could have retired to Monte Carlo but you chose to help others, and that's what you did." She coughed, as if resetting her own thoughts. She'd never wanted this to be a sentimental meeting, excited though she was at meeting her heroine; no, she wanted this to be business; and business it was. "So, if I may recap. You have the drilling rights, but you can't sell them because you don't own the surgery. If you do sell them you can only sell them to Ms Makepeace who has offered you a pittance. Am I correct?"

"Yes."

"Well, I have not brought you here to stand by and see you get wiped out by that horrible piece of work, I still have an ace left."

"An ace?"

"Yes, you know what one of those is? It's something that wins the game at the last minute. You have pulled one of these out on more than one occasion in order to turn desperate situations round for people, I believe? Let's go back in the sitting room and I shall explain."

She led Petunia back into the little sitting room and revealed still more surprises that, once again, rendered the young woman totally shocked and surprised. Moreover, Mrs Spencer had been transformed and now had the air of a Captain of the Homeguard about to lead a vital new campaign. She even refused to sit down as she revealed her thoughts and the ace that she had held until the very end of the game. She paced up and down as she revealed her suggestions and her strategy. This she backed with something that represented a solid and unassailable guarantee like a Government Gilt-Edged Bond but far more valuable.

The two women talked for some time. Petunia had seen more and more of the real person that lay concealed by one's first impression of an elderly cat lady with little else on her mind. In point of fact Mrs Spencer revealed much more that was at complete variance with that hastily-formed view. Moreover, she had clearly been thinking things through for some time and had some crucial proposals of her own to put to Petunia upon whom more and more surprises landed like waves rolling onto a gently sloping beach.

Suddenly, Bobby the ginger tom ran inside, his fur bristling with distress.

"Oh what's going on here? Something or someone has scared poor Bobby.

Excuse me a second, Petunia?"

She got up and left the room. She reported back almost immediately after discovering the source of Bobby's distress.

"Oh it's that dreadful reporter, the one who's been revelling in poor Dr Binder's discomfort."

"Who's that?"

"Oh he's the man from the *Horwich Chronicle* – Dave Scoggins."

"Dave Scoggins!" Petunia's eyes lit up at the mention of a familiar name.

"Yes, and he's snooping round outside."

The old lady held her finger to her lips, "Shhh, he will hear us."

Petunia smiled and whispered to Matilda as she closed the gap between them.

"Can we play a little trick on Mr Scoggins, do you think?"

The older lady laughed. "I think it would be a great waste not to, don't you think? What have you got in mind?"

"It's like being at school again," suggested Petunia, mysteriously.

"It won't mean detention for us will it? Tee hee, I can't wait," concluded Matilda as Petunia whispered again to her.

Petunia now raised her voice and projected it to the open side door, the one Bobby had just rushed through.

"Yes, Matilda, the whole place will go up. It should be quite an explosion. I've deliberately timed it for the opening of the new surgery. The whole building is rigged to blow."

"Oh my, that's delightful," offered Matilda as she choked back her giggles. "That should show them that you mean business."

"Yes, I don't think it will be lost on anyone. Especially with it all exploding in the centre of Horwich. I think it will light up the sky for miles around. The whole thing will go up with a real bang. They'll never suspect, until boom, and off it goes."

Dave Scoggins could neither believe his ears, nor his luck. Not only did he have an exposé about the failing surgery to his name, but he now had, with his own ears, heard about an arson attack on the new surgery, timed deliberately to go off the night the surgery opened. There wasn't much time as the opening was not too far off. He thought quickly, there was just enough time for him to request the front page. He stole away quickly. He needed to get his copy ready.

He quietly slipped away, under cover of darkness, to find his car. He had another massive scoop to write and with it would come his ascendance from these quiet backwater papers and hopefully on to something more commensurate with his manifest skills. This time, it really was time.

Mrs Spencer watched with some merriment as he drove away. She was giggling like a schoolgirl.

"Well, that should put a spoke in his wheel."

"I'd better make sure that the place really does go up, then, opening night."

The two women spent a little time discussing their strategy for development of the new site and also the costs and guarantees that would be embodied within such a deal.

Eventually Petunia hugged the older woman and went off to find her Mini, and her husband who waited restlessly for her.

"Wow, you've been gone a long time."

"And have I got lots to tell you. You want a wee again?"

"Let's just say that prickly bush was looking ever more enticing. Well, you certainly seem to be a lot brighter, so I can't wait."

"What? For a wee?"

"Well yes, that, but I meant, can't wait for you to tell me what's happened. I think I even saw your old friend Dave Scoggins drive past."

"Okay then, let's get going and I can update you as you drive. Suffice to say that Mrs Spencer is not all she seems. She is the one who sent me the letter and she's just given me an ace."

"An ace?"

"Oh, yes, and I will explain exactly how we are going to play it as you drive."

The off-white mini, once again, made hurried and erratic progress up the long lane that led to the main road and the bus stop. The tall, handsome man was amazed by what he heard. So much so, he even forgot about his full bladder.

CHAPTER XVI

Deadlock

A few days later, Petunia waited to see Felix Wertheim, CEO of Carob Oil and Gas. He'd kept her waiting for half an hour but when he eventually appeared, Petunia followed him into his office with the precise rhythmical clip coming from her heels as she did so.

She smoothed the fine wool skirt carefully as she sat facing him. Her features bright, friendly and enthusiastic.

Felix had clearly decided to take a very different tack in their meeting. His features remained unsmiling and taciturn. He made no attempt to restrain his eyes from staring either at her legs or her chest. She returned his gaze but refused to be intimidated or to be made uncomfortable under his penetrating stare. His voice, rather deep and flat, carried something of uncaring menace. It had taken him all his time to shake her hand and he then delivered a bone-crushing handshake that left the poor girl wincing in pain, something he seemed to delight in.

"I know who you are," he began, "and I think it's rather quaint what you do." She only realised later that this meagre attempt to be affable was as warm as he got and his features, as he continued, became even less welcoming. She remained unintimidated but felt rather sorry for someone who obviously spent his life, and his skills, emanating such feelings. He clearly had no warmth to give.

He then went on, "You must realise, however, that I live in the *real* world; that of the hard-headed business deal. I have

responsibilities not only to those who work for me like Ms
Makepeace, whom I believe you have already met," he offered
with no attempt now at defeating the self-satisfied smile that
had appeared, "but also to myself and of course to my board
and shareholders. I run this company as that; a *business*, and I
have no time for someone playing at being the do-gooder who
interferes in the dealings of others." The mask had well and
truly slipped at this point and he now glared unpleasantly at
the young woman whose neutral and impassive bright-blue
eyes met his rather darker gaze unflinchingly. He continued,
"You are well aware of the deal that has been offered to you.
Please do not come here and waste my time. I am not
interested in any sort of bargaining or pleading. You have
made your bed, now you must lie on it."

"Come now, Mr Wertheim, you are being rather coy. You
and a family trust own almost ninety per cent of Carob Oil and
Gas and I believe the dividend structure, whilst in no way
illegal, allows you to pay yourselves directly in dividends
thereby avoiding paying large tranches of income tax and
national insurance."

"So, lots of people do this and as you say there is nothing
illegal in it. Are you trying to insinuate otherwise?"

"Not at all, Mr Wertheim, but I do wish to establish who
are the main beneficiaries of the hard-headed business deals of
which you speak."

"Look, I told you there is no point in coming here and
trying to get us to raise our offer. We have made what must be
seen as a generous settlement of 1p in the pound." Once again
the cruel smile that visited his face so readily appeared. He
looked at his watch. "No, sorry it seems that that deal has now
expired. We are now talking about a tenth of a penny in the
pound. I can give you £180,000 today and you will hand over
all rights to the land in question. This deal will be available
until close of business, five pm tonight. Following this we will
withdraw even this offer. I have a cheque here made out to
what I think is your *real* name?"

"I own the land and all the drilling rights, Mr Wertheim."
She reminded him gently.

"And so you do. And might I remind you they are
worthless without access, which we have acquired." He
almost spat the words. "Take the deal, and let us get on with
proper business and not trying to weave fairy tale endings for
people who amount to nothing. Take our generous offer which
I am sure is still rather a lot of money, to someone like you."
He completed the sentence after a deliberate pause as he made
a further attempt to intimidate the young woman. "Take it,
take it now and please get out of my sight." He now held out a
cheque, almost throwing it at her, which presumably was for
the amount in question. She held out her hand and took it from
him. His cruel smile re-appeared for a further outing, but this
was to be its last such appearance.

As she looked at him her eyes had taken on much more of
an icy hue as they continued to survey him. Slowly she placed
the cheque back on the desk and smiled with more warmth
than he deserved.

"Thank you, you have been most generous. But I agree, Mr
Wertheim, we need to discuss hard-headed business."

"Just cut the crap. Take the money before you are
bankrupted and let me get on with what I do best. I am a busy
man. I have a real business to run. Take the deal, before I
change my mind. You'll still have the clothes on your back
and you can remove yourself from my sight completely."

"My goodness, Mr Wertheim, so much anger. I can see
why you and Ms Makepeace get on so well."

"I am not here to trade pleasantries or to blow smoke up
your butt. Do you want the money or not? If not, then please
leave."

Both people in the room harboured very strong feelings.
The young woman had channelled hers in the way she thought
would best give vent to the heartbreak and energy that was
locked inside her and that, of course, was to help others. Felix
on the other hand had harnessed the feelings within and

allowed them to feed back on themselves thus creating aggression and cruelty. He was now so stuck in his ways that it was unlikely he would ever change.

Ultimately, the young woman realised this.

"I see we are not getting very far, Mr Wertheim. The deal that *is* on the table is as follows. I require two hundred million for the land in question to include the gas and oil bearing land as shown on these plans and access to that land."

He interrupted her almost shouting, "Look, you are in no position to even suggest a deal like that. I've told you what's on the table. I think your do-gooding spell has addled your brain. I don't think you realise what's in play here. You bought an asset of which you failed to gain full control. That has, and is about to, cost you dear. Take the cheque and sign here and then please go."

She smiled pleasantly enough but the rich blue eyes had plummeted in the colour spectrum and now took on the appearance of hard ice. "Quite the contrary, Mr Wertheim, it is you who have bought an asset which you do not control. As we shall see," she pushed some deeds across the table, "A lady called Mrs Spencer sold the surgery to Dr Binder some years ago. This is what you purchased from him. You can see, however, that it did not include the approach road, the road that leads down to the surgery or the access from the main road. She retains ownership of all these. Even the bus stop is rented to the council so that buses can stop off the main road. Our terms are as follows. We require the sum of two-hundred million for the oil-bearing plot and to include the land I discussed a moment ago together with the approach road layby at the top of the road. In addition, you are to purchase from Dr Rapace the surgery in Horwich town centre and leave it in trust for Dr Binder, his partners and his successors. Also, you are to agree to the following terms as regards the comfort and safety of Mrs Spencer and each and every one of her cats. Furthermore, you are to place the sum of one million pounds in trust for Mrs Spencer as security against any future problems she might encounter as a result of releasing the access road to you and your company." She pushed another piece of paper over the desk. "Lastly, you are to make sure that funds are transferred," she looked at her watch, "within two weeks of the current time and date. Am I clear Mr Wertheim?"

"You plucky little bitch, we'll never agree to those terms. You take this cheque and you take it now or you'll be lucky to still have the bus fare home."

"Then, in that case, Mr Wertheim, the bus fare will have to do. That, I believe, concludes our meeting. I am leaving now but my solicitor, Mr Finkelman, is waiting outside. If he leaves here today without your agreement to our terms, which have now become non-negotiable, then we will simply leave things as they are and I shall retain ownership of the land."

Ultimately, as all deal-makers knew, the person who won the argument was the one who was first prepared to walk away. He saw that the young woman was perfectly happy to do such a thing even though it would mean significant loss of funds for her. He realised now that she'd rather face ruin that be bullied into signing an agreement with him.

She stood, "Good day to you, Mr Wertheim. I will send Mr Finkelman in and you can then decide if you are going to accept our proposals or otherwise. I should advise you that Mr Finkelman is not empowered to change the nature of the deal I have just put to you. Your choice is a simple one, either take the deal that I have outlined, or we will cease to waste each other's time. Good day." She turned and walked out of his office, without subjecting her right hand to further pain. She handed a piece of paper to her solicitor and advised him these were the only terms she was prepared to accept. Mr Finkelman rose quickly and nodded to her as he gave her a bemused smile. He then went in to see Mr Wertheim, whose face had now taken on a very different expression.

Felix had looked carefully at her as she departed without so much as a further glance in his direction. She had seen through him completely and detected that he needed this land and the deal that she had offered if he was to secure the future viability of Carob Oil and also his own position. One recurring theme would come to haunt him in the days ahead. In this time, and for months to come, the whole company would struggle with severe cashflow problems as they desperately waited for the gas and oil to flow; so much so, that they were in danger of breaching their banking covenants.

He considered, as he struggled to concentrate during the day and get some sleep at night, that if he had been kinder and less abrasive with the young woman, then more favourable terms might have been made available to him. Indeed, on the afternoon of their meeting, Mr Finkelman as he came in after Petunia had left, gave a hint that such a thing might have been possible. Mr Finkelman read and digested the note that she'd given him and made sure that all the relevant points were agreed. Although such insight would indeed occur to the oil executive in the weeks ahead, he missed the wider point that the rage that existed within him could never have made possible such a thing as his proper treatment of another.

CHAPTER XVII

Time To Shine

The following morning Petunia took an early call from Mr Finkelman.

"Good morning. I can confirm that we are successful. I have insisted on the deal that you outlined to me. I have informed Mr Wertheim that no further negotiation is in the offing; he takes this deal or nothing. Mercifully, he saw sense and we managed to draft the full agreement yesterday, which he signed. I will send you a copy and please let me know if there is anything further you require?"

"Oh no, Mr Finkelman, you have been most efficient and most kind, as always. Please let me have your fee note at your earliest convenience and I will ask Mr Bloor to settle your invoice at once. I am so grateful to you for your working so quickly."

"I was aware of the fact that their cash flow predictions are really tight and in truth this played directly into our hands. When I explained that I was not at liberty to change your instructions, he signed without delay. If I may say so, he is a rather unpleasant character. I can see why you chose not to stay."

"Well, in truth, the more I said the more he took exception to. I reasoned that the only thing he was going to pay attention to was a time limited and 'take it or leave it' deal."

"It seems this is the only type of business he transacts, only usually it comes from his side giving the ultimatum."

"Always, always, this must be a first for him. Thank you again, Mr Finkelman for helping me."

"That is my absolute pleasure, as always, and might I be permitted to say how pleased I am that you managed to turn events in your favour? I should have been most upset to see you fail."

"Thank you for that. It was a close-run thing, I am sure I don't have to tell you, but we live to fight another day and our work will go on."

"I am so pleased to see that. Please look out for the courier who will be with you within the hour."

A little later Petunia waited patiently outside the front door of the little terraced house just off the main street that ran through Horwich.

Once again, the rather obese man with the string vest came to the door but, apart from looking the young woman up and down, said nothing. He did glance, once again, at the Cartier sitting elegantly on her slim wrist and thought, as he did so, that on this occasion it seemed entirely commensurate with the rest of her appearance. The only concession he made to this was another grunt that was at a slightly higher pitch than the one he'd produced the first time he'd seen her. As he turned his back on her, leaving her standing on the threshold, he did call to his daughter as he moved away. Petunia did her best to avoid the image of his bulging natal cleft from assaulting her vision too much.

"Sue, 's'that woman again for you."

Susan came to the door and looked surprised.

"Hello Petunia, I didn't expect to see you again. You look fabulous, just love your hair."

"Thank you, you are very kind. One or two things have been keeping me busy, but I think we have things back on track now."

"Look, I told you, you don't owe me anything. We tried, we failed, it's over. Nothing more needs to be said and you don't need to come here with more apologies or more money that the news says you haven't got."

Petunia smiled, but said nothing at this point.

"Look, I have the chance of a job at the new Aldi that's opening. I am number two hundred and seventy-five in the queue."

"And how long is the queue?"

"Fifty."

Petunia nodded slowly.

"Actually, Susan, I came to give you this," she held out a little plastic card about the size of a credit card which had a magnetic strip down one side and a chip embedded in its surface.

"What's this?"

"It's a thousand pounds."

Susan looked at the card a little hungrily but nevertheless moved to return it to her visitor, "Look, I told you, I don't want your money or your charity. Don't feel bad and don't feel guilty, but I have my pride and sooner or later I will get another job," a frisson of fear crossed her expression as she almost turned to look back into the little house.

Petunia smiled again but did not accept the card, "Oh, it isn't charity, I can promise you that." She nodded with the certainty of her actions. "It's a down payment on the wages that you'll be earning in your *new* job. You'll be expected to work for that amount in hours and then your salary will kick in, *if* you can hack it."

"A job?"

"A job." Petunia nodded again.

"But doing what, exactly?" although she still held out the card, her grip tightened upon it ever so slightly as she sensed it was to be hers all along; and that she'd earn it in honest graft.

"Oh, something I think you are rather good at: something that will come as second nature to you. Something that will give you what you want – the chance to shine. Only problem is, I need a few more. How many of you did Amanda Makepeace force out?"

"Including Tina Bessemer and me there were ten in total."

"Oh, I have already spoken with Tina. Funny, she has a new job offer, too." Petunia's beguiling smile rose in the gloom of the wintry and grey day that seemed to exist over Horwich like the permafrost. "Are you still in touch with the other eight?"

Susan nodded but now began to look a little overwhelmed.

"Here are eight more cards, for the others. Please tell them that there is a job waiting for each of them but they will be expected to work hours to the value of the card and then, if they wish, they will be offered a permanent role."

"But, but doing what exactly?"

"I told you, something that I believe, given the chance, you will all be rather good at. This is that chance and it's *time* to shine."

"But doing what exactly?"

"Watch the local news tomorrow and you will see."

Susan now held the card firmly and moved it a little closer. "I suspect I should be thanking you. I suspect you have done what I, in my wildest of dreams, hoped you would."

"It wasn't without help, quite a lot of help, and it was a bit touch and go. Watch the news and all will become clear."

"Thank you, thank you so much. I am going to tell my Dad I have a new job?"

"Yes, I would do that. There is also a job for him if he would like?"

"Doing what? Oh yes, I know I am going to have to watch the news."

Petunia smiled by way of reply.

"What do I call you? It isn't Petunia, is it? Not really."

"I'd like for you very much to call me a friend?"

"*Friend* it is."

The tears formed slowly in both women's eyes. By way of reply, Susan came forward and gave her visitor a hug. Petunia handed Susan a piece of paper. "Here is my number. If you like what you see on the news, then you'll know what to do.

Training begins as soon as the news ends. One or two have already begun training so that they can train others and you may well see a little more on the news tomorrow. Certainly, you will see one person you'll recognise immediately."

"I can't wait, it sounds really exciting."

"Yes, I was hoping you'd say that; and the fun is only just beginning."

"Thank you, Petunia."

"I'm sorry, it was such a close call and I thought that I'd failed you all."

"Not from where I am standing."

Susan hugged her again. Petunia then turned with no more words being spoken and went to find the off-white Mini that waited for her down the road. Just as she did so she heard Susan's excited squeal as she rushed inside to tell her parents the news.

Susan switched on the local breakfast news the following day as did a great many others. Like Susan, more than a few now had a vested interest in what was to be revealed that day. The reporter stood outside the old cinema in Horwich town centre. Builders' vans were parked in front and the whole façade was adorned with scaffolding. Delivery lorries appeared dropping off building material and supplies in order to refurbish the building for its new purpose and get it up and running as quickly as possible. Other lorries came to collect rubble and waste that had been ripped out in order to create a very different working space from that originally intended. While the reporter made her broadcast, tens and tens of workmen seemed to be working frantically in order to move things on as quickly as possible.

The lights flared, the sound booms were activated and the producer called for hush from the chattering production team as he gave the countdown on his fingers for the live broadcast to begin. One or two bemused pedestrians hurried awkwardly past as the cameras flared. The producer glared at each of them as if daring them to spoil his piece. The reporter stood there with a fixed smile stuck on her face as she waited for him to point the final finger. There it was upon her.

"I am standing in front of the Horwich cinema. Or, perhaps, I should say the former cinema. Many of you will know that it was closed some years ago and has lain idle, deserted and boarded up since that time. However, as you can see from the bustling activity behind me, the cinema has new owners with ambitious plans to turn it into a modern GP surgery, so badly needed by the local populace. We are told that the contractors are working double shifts, round the clock, in order to open the new surgery as soon as possible."

"I am joined by Dr Binder, senior partner and custodian of the new building."

The camera angle widened a little and a somewhat embarrassed Neil Binder blinked a little uncertainly under the bright lighting which did its best to push back yet another grey, blustery day in the West Pennine town.

"Thank you for joining us, Dr Binder. Congratulations on your new appointment. If I might ask, however, is it true that the CQC closed your last surgery down as a result of poor performance?"

"Yes, that is perfectly true and it's also true that another doctor planned to open here and provide General Medical Services to the local folk. When his plans fell through, owing to lack of funds, I was approached to see if I could take over the project which has been funded by the unselfish generosity of some very kind, hard-working and generous people who have made all this possible. I am also asked to mention Carob Oil and Gas who have contributed massively to the project which will be owned and held in trust by an independent body. In addition, the CQC and NHS England have allowed me to open as soon as the building work will allow."

"Is it also true, Dr Binder, that you are effectively retained on a trial basis and that you are to be inspected within the next three months?"

"Yes, that is quite correct. My tenure here is at all times to be based on my performance and of course the feedback from, and the quality of the service we provide to, the patients."

"I am told of problems at your previous surgery?"

"That is also correct, but I would beg people to consider that that is all behind us now."

"How can you be sure of that?"

"Very simple. If I do not perform and I do not provide the standard of care that the CQC and Clinical Care Authority expect of me, then I will be summarily dismissed and other doctors brought in. The focus here is on the patients and they will soon be able to judge for themselves." At this point, Dr Binder stared directly at the camera which had zoomed in.

"Can I ask you, are you confident that you will be able to perform to the required standard?"

Once again, he looked directly at the camera. "I *am* confident. We have new premises with every modern facility. I have loyal, hard working, tried and tested staff who have stuck by me and I have been backed by kind, generous people who have risked everything in order to get me, and this surgery, back on track. The staff have also had, and continue to have, some excellent and expert training on the new systems. I am not planning on letting them, myself, or the patients down. I simply ask that people judge us by what they see from *today* and, hopefully, forgive some of the mistakes of the past."

"Is it true that you have been helped by Poppy Dixon, the girl who won the highest-ever prize in the EuroMillions."

"It wouldn't be right for me to comment on this one way or the other but I can confirm that without the unceasing patience, kindness and generosity of others, I would not be talking to you today."

"Last question, then, Dr Binder. How can patients register?"

"We have a temporary booth set up just over there where patients can attend personally," the camera panned round to reveal a steady queue of patients waiting to register, "or they can register online via the CCG website or by telephoning them. The number has been posted outside the building. My staff, most of whom have worked with me before, are being trained in the new premises as we speak and as the builders free up some office space."

"Well then, Dr Binder, that's all we need to know. Thank you for appearing on Breakfast this morning and we wish you the best of fortune."

The camera cut back to the GP who nodded and thanked the reporter. Those watching in High-Definition would be able to see a little moisture collecting in the corner of each of his eyes just as the cameras focussed once again on the reporter.

"As you can see behind me there seems to be a lot of interest in the new surgery." The camera once again cut to the queue of patients waiting to register. "It remains to be seen if Dr Binder can prove his critics wrong, and provide the standard of medical care that the local area has been crying out for. Back to the studio."

Some of those watching stared, feeling numb. Some wept just a few tears and some danced round the room as they watched and heard what their old boss had to say.

Susan did none of those things but she looked at the plastic card that had been loaded with funds to the value of one thousand pounds. She turned it slowly between her thumb, index and middle finger as she did so. After a slight pause, she spoke to her father.

"Looks like she came through, Dad." He snorted by way of reply.

"She says there's a job for you too, Dad, if you'd like? I'm going to phone now and get some of this training. Shall I make some enquiries about you?"

"What do they want an old duffer like me for? I'm finished."

"You are fifty-four, Dad, and she told me there's a job there for you, if you'd like one. I'm going to ask anyway when I start my training and you can decide then. That new surgery, full of new stuff and with Dr Binder in charge, it's just what we need."

"They say he's kaput, like me, say he died the day of that accident."

"Well, you saw him being interviewed, like me, and like me you might be thinking otherwise, right now?" Susan looked thoughtfully at the TV and then at her mobile phone. She was going to call the number she'd been given. She'd also handed out the cards that Petunia had left with her and suspected that all the others would be making a call too.

"New job, Dad. Would make a fresh start for us both?" Once again Susan's father snorted a little as he continued to watch the television. He didn't look at her but, on this occasion, his left eyebrow was raised just a little with a flicker of curiosity that had been generated.

CHAPTER XVIII

New Beginnings

The following week the surgery was ready for its official opening. The Mayor attended to cut the bright crimson ribbon but the special guest was Mrs Spencer. All the girls were in attendance and were wearing their new uniforms. Some of the builders remained and only one consulting room was available but they'd promised that three more would be finished within the next few days. The opening had attracted a lot of interest and the local TV had returned to film the events of the day.

A series of powered sliding doors, in glass, had been fitted to the entrance and these were in constant motion as people came and went; only their slight whirring betrayed their labours. Leading on from the small vestibule was the large, bright and airy reception and waiting room. The back office could be seen beyond the reception desk bathed in both natural and man-made illumination. LED emitters had been set in the ceiling at regular intervals and these shone a bright white light to reflect off the white walls and gleaming chrome and glass surfaces. Impactful pictures of local scenes had been commissioned and hung at regular intervals along the walls to add interest and to break up the clinical air.

The sleek, white reception desk, with glass work-surfaces, gleamed in the overhead lighting. Large, bright, flat screens swivelled on perfectly balanced booms mounted on the fitted desks and new keyboards sat ready, each with a modern cordless mouse adjacent to it. State of the art computer terminals communicated effortlessly with a leading-edge fileserver which pulsated smoothly in an air-conditioned cupboard upstairs. This in turn was connected via high-speed fibre-optic pathways to national NHS systems and remote servers situated in data centres hundreds of miles away. Susan looked up as Petunia arrived.

"That is a sight for sore eyes," Petunia said, as even her bright features seemed barely able to contain her smile.

"I agree and it's all thanks to you. I'm just waiting for some more instruction on the new computer system from your husband."

"Yes, this is the bit he really enjoys, staff training. You really look the part, Susan, welcome to where you were always meant to be." She hugged the new receptionist.

"I promise we won't let you down, or him. She nodded to the glass-etched plates that contained Dr Binder's name. You've given us all a chance to be the very best we can be."

"I know that. Did your dad say anything about the Pharmacy?"

"Yes, he said that he'd be delighted to be their delivery driver, if they'll have him? My mum is ecstatic; she'll have the house back to herself again."

In that moment Dr Binder strode in, his face brighter than any of the girls had seen it in the recent past. He was overjoyed to see so many familiar faces.

"Petunia, just how could you have done all this?"

"Well, Dr Binder, I don't think I could have done any of this without more than a little luck, and more than a little help from a person you know well. Here she comes. Hello, Mrs Spencer, welcome. Dr Binder and I were just going to have a look round, would you like to come too?"

Wild horses could not have restrained the older lady at this point. She came forward and hugged Dr Binder and then Petunia.

She linked Petunia's arm. "I knew you could do it, Petunia," she began, her eyes darting around as she took in more and more of the inner décor of the surgery on which no expense had been spared.

"Not without you, Matilda. You have made all this possible, not me."

"Oh nonsense, I don't think that for a moment. I am just the one who wrote a letter." She offered with a mischievous look appearing on her expression.

"Oh, I think you did a lot more than that, and here we are."

"This has cost a pretty penny, I'm guessing."

"Yes, Carob Oil were more than co-operative when we'd explained one or two harsh realities to them. They agreed to underwrite all the costs of the new building and its conversion."

"I bet they didn't have a choice did they?" asked the elderly lady, a wicked smile now replacing the mischievous one.

"No, not really!" confirmed Petunia.

"I believe they even paid Dr Rapace out at full value," added Matilda, the impish look being re-invigorated, "Not that that will do him any good. He's up to his neck in an expensive divorce and he is having to do locum work just to stay afloat."

Dr Binder pulled Petunia to one side.

"Petunia, who are you? Are you the person they say you are? They say you are an ex-receptionist who won the biggest-ever lottery prize and who uses it to the benefit of others."

She paused, the limitless cerulean of her eyes focussed on the GP, "I told you who I am. I am just a friend; a friend who came to help you and deliver you from some pretty evil people who never had your interests at heart, unlike these people who *all* have your interests at heart." She swept her arm through a long arc as she pointed to the staff and some of the patients who'd drifted in. "All these people never stopped believing in you. Maybe it's time for you to believe in yourself, Dr Binder."

"I am going to give it my very best shot. And if I don't, they'll soon have me out of here!"

She smiled, "Oh, I don't think that's going to happen. I think you won't look back and all your reception staff are dedicated to making both this place, and you, a great success."

"I'm just a bit frightened we have had so many people register. I think we will be swamped. I may have to offer Dr Rapace a job to help me."

"Oh, well that's for you to decide, though I hear that he is rather busy with a very acrimonious divorce."

"And look at these computers, how will the girls cope with all this new tech?"

"Please don't worry, the staff are all ready and have got up to speed with the new systems," she beckoned to the tall man who was busy on the other side of the room. He came over.

"Meet my husband, Tom, Dr Binder." The tall man shook the GP's hand. "We have been running intensive training for all the staff while we were waiting for the building to be ready. They are a nice group of girls and they are keen to learn and keen to show what they can do. I think you can be very proud of them, Dr Binder, I know I am. They are just about ready," said the tall man with the chestnut brown eyes that glowed with capability, fairness and purpose. "If you have an hour this afternoon, I can give you some training, too. Otherwise, I think you are just about ready to open, Dr Binder."

"Tom, thank you so much for all you have done. Please call me Neil. It's all a bit daunting, I think we'll need some help."

Just out of the corner of her eye, Petunia saw a young woman rushing in as soon as the glass doors parted.

"Oh, Neil, if I could re-introduce you to an old friend of yours, Tina Bessemer?"

"Tina!"

"Hello, Dr Binder."

He began by shaking her hand but then couldn't resist hugging her. Petunia smiled at them both. "I wondered if Tina would be interested in the job of practice manager? It will take some of the weight off your shoulders and she is well known to you and the other staff as well. She's already been trained on the new computer system."

"Oh, yes please, perfect. That's if you can possibly forgive me?"

The new manager smiled. She paused for a moment because she recognised a look in his eyes that she'd not seen for many years. Only then did she reply.

"Without a doubt, I think there's every possibility of that, Dr Binder. The other problem is shortage of medical staff. I am sure it's a nice problem to have in many ways. So many patients have followed us to the new surgery."

"Followed you all to the new surgery," confirmed Petunia, whilst Matilda and Tina looked on.

"Well, we can cope with locums for the time being but one or two new partners would underpin the place."

While they had been talking a red Nissan Micra had parked in front of the new surgery. A young doctor got out of the car and came in through the glass doors which whisked apart quickly and quietly to allow her access. She recognised the person she'd come to meet but knew who at least one of the other persons was. Petunia turned round and smiled as the female doctor approached.

"Oh, Dr Binder, right on cue. May I introduce you to Dr Waller, who is a friend of mine and someone who is looking for a new opportunity?"

Dr Waller offered a slim hand and Dr Binder eagerly grabbed it.

"Perhaps if the two of you enjoy working together then you may both wish to make it more permanent?"

"I'd like nothing more, Petunia," he said but did not take his eyes from the female doctor.

Dr Waller seemed surprised at the mention of a name she did not recognise but then thought of very different things. She hugged Tom as he stood there.

"Well, Dr Binder, that sounds great. Perhaps a look round and I can start as soon as?"

Petunia left Dr Binder talking to the Mayor and Matilda. She walked round the new surgery with Dr Waller and Tina.

Susan Waller began, "Wow, just as you said, he is quite a dish."

"Hey, hands off. I saw him first," said Tina.

"Ok then, Tina, may the best girl win," suggested Susan; her eyes narrowed playfully as she focussed on the new manager.

"Now, you two aren't going to come to blows are you, just when we've got this place on track?"

"No, I'm sure we'll be the best of friends, and I promise a fair fight and we'll see who can win him over," said Tina.

"I think the attention will do Dr Binder some good. I can see he'll be in good hands with you two," replied Petunia.

"What's this, *Petunia*, anyway?" asked Dr Waller.

"Oh, it's a bit of a long tale but I suspect you'll have guessed much of it."

"Ah yes, I see, *Julia*," she said with a smile.

Petunia left the new staff to wander round. She paused, for a moment, just to take in the surroundings and to sample the bright thoughts that seemed to permeate throughout. Of course, the future was an unknown quantity but with good staff who'd been liberated from under the lash of their previous, cruel manager, as well as a resurgent senior partner, she could only think that the omens were good. The tall man was busy in the office with final training and running up the new systems. Most of the girls caught on very quickly and were keen to learn. He in turn was an excellent, patient and thorough teacher, something she'd always known.

Petunia went to sit behind the large, curved, white desk on reception. Reflective thoughts were always encouraged by a little quiet and solitude. It reminded her tantalisingly of old times and more than this as she stared directly ahead at the new banks of patient seats that had just been installed. Glass panels with gaps between them came down from the ceiling and lights set into the ceiling illuminated the glass and the bright-chromed fittings. She smiled to herself as she considered that the new, shining fittings and surroundings could only send the strongest signal of new beginnings well removed from the dark, miserable days of the past.

Emma Sparkle approached.

"Plenty to keep you busy here, Mrs Sparkle. But at least it's all new and shiny."

"Right you are, girlie. Dr Binder says he'll be needing a new cleaner or two and it seemed mad not to take up his kind offer, especially as it's now only two minutes from my house.

Had a wonderful visit at my home from a banker of all things – he says it's all mine. I thought he'd come to fore…, fore…, turn me out. Instead he produces a cheque for twenty five thousand and says it really is all mine and, you know, for once a banker that tells the truth – it was. Can you believe that eh, girlie?"

"Well, that's simply wonderful, Emma. I am so pleased for you. You are now secure in your own home."

"Don't s'pose you know anything about that, do you?"

"I don't think I do, Emma, but it sounds like good news."

A pause opened up as Emma stared at the young woman.

"I owe you an apology, girlie."

"You do? Why is that Emma?"

"I was a bit hard on you and him over there, that tall laddo." She pointed to the tall chap still teaching the new staff. "Truth be told, I never thought you'd deliver all this. Never thought for a moment." Her speech drifted a little as she looked round at the splendour of the new surgery. "Anyways, I want you to know I am sorry. I underestimated you and 'im for sure."

"Well, Emma, you didn't say anything that wasn't true, nor anything that I hadn't said to myself, and it was all stuff I needed to hear. Besides, I don't think we could have done any of this without Mrs Spencer," she said, nodding in the older lady's direction.

"That's as maybe, girlie, but I don't think she could've

done any of this without a very special person. That's why she wrote to you."

"I am hoping that they've all been given a fresh start."

"Look at 'im, what've you done to 'im?" she nodded to Dr Binder. "seems he's stepped outta that grave at last," she said, lowering her voice, although there was so much chatter that it was unlikely even Emma Sparkle's tones would carry.

"Me? Nothing."

"You're very modest, girlie, reckon you've 'ad an 'and in lots'a things 'ere and elsewhere, so they tell me. Well, someone's firing that pulse of 'is. First time I've seen 'im smile in five years. Look at them two young women. I reckon it might be a fresh start for 'im too."

"I certainly hope so, I think it's time."

"'Ave you noticed that ring 'as gone, too."

"Yes, I've seen it's missing."

The cleaner then pointed to the receptionists nearby. "Look at them, they look like a team for the very first time and it will be a pleasure to work among them. Seems I won't be cleanin' for nothin' any more." Finally she nodded over at Tom, "'E's done wonders with 'em that 'andsome chap of yours. Don't tell him that, he'll get big headed. Look at the way them girls look at 'im"

"Oh, I think that'll do him good, having one or two eyes on him, he doesn't get out much."

"Don't s'pose there's any possibility of you two staying?"

"No, sorry, Mrs S, once our work is done we move on, though I have promised to visit and when I do I will seek you out."

"You be good and promise me that then. Kind'a thought you were gonna say that, but I can say it's been a pleasure."

Emma held out her hand but the former receptionist bypassed this and gave her a hug.

"I've promised to keep in touch with Mrs Spencer so if you need anything just let me know and I'll call on you and maybe we can have a nice cuppa?"

"I'd like that but don't worry about me, I think, somehow, you've done far too much for me already. You and that 'andsome banker you sent to call on me."

The tall chap walked over.

"Well that's them just about sorted. I think Tina will get the hang of it very quickly though the system suppliers will give her more formal training on the data reports. I'm hoping that those reports will soon start reflecting the changes that have taken place here," Tom said.

"Time for us to leave?" Petunia asked.

She linked her arm with his.

"Just one minute fella, can't let you go without a hug from me," insisted Mrs Sparkle.

A somewhat over enthusiastic kiss was planted on his cheek. She turned to the young woman and winked at her behind his back 'Wow!' she mouthed.

The young couple walked towards the door.

As they did so they found a policeman waiting for them.

Excuse me, Miss, but we've been alerted by the *Horwich Chronicle* about a threat of arson to the new surgery."

"Arson, officer? Just who would do such a thing?"

"Well it's plastered on their front page. Super said I should check things over. The article was penned by their chief reporter, Dave Scoggins. He's hiding over there but I wasn't s'posed to tell you that. He says the whole place 'as been rigged, like."

"Oh, I nearly forgot," smiled Petunia. "It's nearly time. Outside everyone, please," she raised her voice above the excited crowd.

The policeman looked especially worried at this point as the young woman had not made any attempt to deny any of the reports that had been plastered on the front page of the *Chronicle*.

Dave Scoggins waited on the far side of the street but at a safe distance. He had a couple of photographers with him ready for any eventuality. He was delighted when he saw everyone run out of the new building; his discovery about dark deeds on opening day must be correct. How pleased he was that he'd shouted down his editor to run with the story and put it on the front page. This was, without doubt, another scoop for him. Time to think of that move to London after all and most sweet of all he'd got his revenge on Poppy Dixon and that grammar school lad who thought he was something.

So many people rushed from the building it could only be that the bomb threat was real. He was glad that he'd insisted on his name being displayed prominently just under the article and that he would be forever associated with another blistering scoop.

Petunia went to find Mrs Spencer and stood with her on the pavement as the excitement and air of expectation built.

"Petunia, I am so pleased you were able to bring all this about."

"*We* were able to bring it about, Matilda. As I said, I couldn't have done this without you. Are the arrangements with Carob Oil working out?"

"Oh yes, thanks to the penalty clauses that Mr Finkelman built in to the contract. They are as quiet as church mice and stick to the agreed hours of working and even look out for my cats. They transferred a million pounds to me. That can't be right?"

"Well, they were so mean when I went in there I thought I'd ask for a little extra. Tuck that money away as it is your insurance policy in case you have to move or if any other unforeseen eventuality occurs."

"Oh, I don't think they will upset me now that your Mr Finkelman has put the fear of God into them. Besides I can't accept the money."

"Matilda, please, I will sleep better in my bed knowing that you are protected. Please?"

"Very well, if it will ensure your sleep. I may just start charitable acts for others, a bit like my heroine."

Petunia laughed, "Very well, but let me get back to Vancouver first, I don't want to be stealing any of your thunder. Come on it's time."

Once everyone had evacuated the building, and under the cover of advancing darkness, Petunia stood on a small platform that the builders had erected. She grabbed Matilda's hand and asked her to come on to the platform with her. "I have the pleasure of introducing Matilda Spencer whose far thinking and generosity has made all this possible. Everyone I'd like to declare the 'Spencer Surgery' open, at least from tomorrow." Petunia hurriedly passed to Matilda a button on a plastic case to which was attached a long wire. The policeman had insisted on accompanying them on to the platform but made no attempt to stop Mrs Spencer from pressing the button. A firework display began, the like of which Horwich had never seen.

Suddenly the whole area erupted; so much so that the whole of the town seemed to be bathed in a fantastic array of flashes over the whole spectrum of light which was accompanied by banging as the fireworks went off against the black of the sky. The amazing display went on for half an hour. Everyone, save one, cheered as it did so. Dave Scoggins was grateful for the noise and the confusion. He used this to quietly slink away hoping that nobody had recognised him. How unfortunate that he'd insisted his picture should accompany the article.

Lastly, hot dog vendors, pizza vans and popcorn and cookie stands appeared and the crowds were encouraged to help themselves free of charge.

In the confusion, the tall chap and Petunia walked slowly away to find the off-white mini parked a little way down the street. Susan saw Petunia leaving and ran after her.

"Petunia, Petunia! I know that's not your real name, is it? But I have it kind'a stuck," she said, as she prodded the side of her own head.

"No, but it's fine with me," Petunia confirmed.

"Look, I just wanted to thank you. We'd all dared to hope that you'd be the one."

Petunia hugged her, "Look, it's my pleasure, and my hope for you now is that you make me as proud as you hope to be of yourself."

"Oh, have no worries on that score. Thanks, too, for finding my dad a job, my mum is delighted. It will stop the two of them from screaming at each other. I think he quite fancies doing a bit of delivering for the pharmacy. He'll be chatting up all the old dears. Meanwhile we, us girls, are going to show everyone just how good a surgery can be, and he has shown us just how to go about it," she nodded to the tall chap.

She turned and walked back leaving them to find their car.

CHAPTER XIX

Flight

Miss Mumple walked over the air bridge and via Door 2 straight in to *First*. Two hostesses waited to greet the passengers who were embarking on the BA flight from Heathrow to Vancouver. A variety of complex sounds washed over her, the most noticeable the slight whirring and hissing from the Rolls-Royce engines as they idled with a slow and gentle rotation preparing for their labours to come.

Melissa's eyes widened with genuine delight. She was the most senior of the hostesses on duty that day.

"Ah, Miss Dixon, I was hoping that it was you, I saw your name had appeared on the flight manifest. We are so pleased to have you on board this morning. Let me show you to your seat. Will you be travelling alone or will Mr Plant be joining you?"

"Tom will be along in a moment. I think he's just wrestling with a rather large moose"

"A moose?" her face filled with puzzlement.

Poppy's eyes rolled upwards, "Don't ask, Melissa, you will only encourage him more. He brings back a soft toy to add to my Aunt's collection every time we travel. I think there won't be enough room in the house for us very soon. I'm going to have to start blindfolding him when we walk through duty-free in future as he seems to find these soft toys and then can't resist them."

"Well, I suppose it could be worse. He could be stocking up on large duty-free chocolate bars."

"Oh, he brings those as well."

"I thought you were about to tell me that congratulations were in order?" she said as she glanced at Poppy's tummy. Melissa smiled, nodded slightly as she acknowledged her mistake and dropped into her more diplomatic mode.

"May I get you anything while you are settling in, madam?"

"Just a glass of orange juice please, Melissa."

"May I take your jacket?"

Her fingers crushed the fabric ever so slightly as she caressed the garment after espying the label. With this, Tom appeared carrying a large toy moose.

"Hello, Mr Plant, nice to see you again. I see you have a new friend, what a lovely purchase. Can we put him in the locker for you, or would you like him on your knee? We can even find a seatbelt for him if you would wish?" Melissa offered carefully.

"No, Melissa thank you, he's just a soft toy, he'll be fine in the locker, perhaps with just a bowl of pumpkin soup?"

His face, which was held completely expressionless, suddenly softened in a laugh. "Only joking, Melissa, he can be stowed anywhere that's convenient for you. My wife's aunt loves soft toys."

"Ah yes, I see. I was asking your wife if maybe congratulations were in order." She queried as she looked at Poppy

"Oh, don't start him off," Poppy's smile was directed briefly at Melissa but mainly at her husband, who stood next to Poppy as he handed over the moose.

"Excuse me, Mr Plant, have you the correct time?"

Tom raised his left arm ostentatiously. He pressed the little silver button on his watch which suddenly sprang to life displaying the array of tiny blue dots arranged in a seemingly indecipherable pattern.

"Yes, Melissa, I *am* glad you asked," he winked at her with delight, "it's 7:43 precisely."

"Thank you, Sir," said the hostess, unable to hide her whimsical smile.

"Just don't ask him to change it to Vancouver time."

They laughed together. He sat down next to Poppy. She smiled weakly at him as he did so.

The young stewardess detected immediately the sadness that had descended on the young woman's face and quickly withdrew. Fortunately, there was much for her to do as she and her colleagues made ready for take off, her disappearance being nicely masked by the rush of activity required of the cabin staff in order to attend to other matters.

He held her hand, sensing something of her fragility. A tiny tear appeared in the corner of her mesmerising blue eyes. He squeezed harder.

"Wow, that was interesting."

"You warned me, told me that it was a potential disaster. Mr Bloor, too, warned me, told me that it was foolhardy."

"And you, my love, went forward anyway, and if I may say, this is what makes you so special. If you had walked away, then they would have lost everything. Your intervention saved them: every single one of them. What's more, might I add, they are very grateful. I am told they wanted to call it the 'Petunia Mumple Surgery', which would have been a bit of a mouthful."

"I am so sorry, Tom. Can you forgive me?"

"What, my love, is there to forgive?"

"I nearly lost everything. In fact, if it hadn't been for Mrs Spencer I *would* have lost everything: everything that we've been working towards. We would also have lost the house in Canada – the whole lot. I don't know what would have become of us and my Aunt, whom I promised to look after. I went in there thinking it was oh so easy. Even when you warned me, I still put everything on the line. It was almost as if I'd gambled the whole lot on a throw of weighted dice."

He laughed, "Well, I wouldn't put it quite as harshly as

that! I've told you that I'll still love you whether you are rich or poor."

"And I've told you that it's whether we are rich or poor."

"Very well, whether we are rich or poor. You know that I fell in love with that wonderful, amazing, but poor, receptionist all those years ago. I know, and I hope you know, that regardless of whether she'd won the lottery or not I'd still love her."

"But I went in there thinking that one click of my fingers would sort it."

Despite the reassuring words sadness continued to inhabit the pretty face.

He turned so that his warm, brown eyes could engage directly with her rather moist blue ones. "You were up against a nasty piece of work. Perhaps you didn't realise just how bad some people are. You always try to see the best in people, to live in the brighter part of your life. Surely then, it's not always possible to see the murky depths that some people routinely plumb. We know that Amanda was such a person and I think she'd have done and said anything to achieve her own ends. He was no better, that Felix chap. He, too, sounds like a nasty piece of work. Perhaps, it boils down to the fact that all those people were expendable to her and him and to you they weren't. You went in there hoping to save them all and she was hoping to destroy them. In the end that's exactly what you did. The only people she cared about were herself and Felix, her boss. Not for the first time, you put others before yourself. Tell me, would you have it any other way?"

"No, but I put them before you and my Aunt. We would have been turned out if Id lost everything."

"I'm sure we would have been okay in a tent in Stanley Park."

"Perhaps it was so close that it nearly came down to that."

"Besides, I'm sure we could have sold the rock."

He touched the 6-carat emerald-cut, solitaire, flawless diamond on her left hand.

"I went in there…"

Her distress wouldn't allow her to carry the words.

She tried again even as the tears beaded, once again, in the corners of her eyes.

"I went in there…" her words failed again. Not that she needed to say more, he knew exactly what she was about to say before her slim fingers moved to touch her neck. The scar to be found there, indicating where they'd inserted a breathing tube in order to ventilate her the night she'd been admitted unconscious after her imprisonment in the house fire. A conflagration that had almost killed her and would surely have done so, had it not been for him.

The tears accumulated in her eyes and his, too, began to sting.

"If you hadn't come for me…" Another sentence that she couldn't complete finished only with a pause.

He squeezed her hand firmly. His expression reached its point of maximum sadness and concern. He chose her words, being the only ones that would serve in that moment.

"Always, always," he offered, as his mellow yet intense brown eyes glanced away for a second from the sadness etched to her expression that was hard for him to bear.

"I'll always come for you, while there is breath in my body, despite the *pickle* you occasionally find yourself immersed in."

"I know." She used the hand that had moved down from her neck to now overlap his. She smiled briefly as she caught the brightening nuances of his expression.

"But, why? Why do I get myself in these *pickles*? Am I nosy, interfering, arrogant …? Her questions tailed off.

"Absolutely, none of those things! You've simply inherited your dad's need to reach the answer, the solution to the puzzle. The complex equation that you see before you, one that demands an answer from you: an answer that you *have* to uncover. It's part of what makes you so special because they are others' problems that you take on! Don't consider it a failing – despite it nearly *killing* you." She joined in the last words as he spoke them.

"In a nutshell, that's you and what you'll always be, I suspect. And why I'll always love you."

She bent down to now kiss the hand that hers had been covering.

Melissa, from the other side of the cabin had done her level best, but failed, not to stare and wonder what had passed between them as her curiosity rose with every expression on their faces and each movement from their lips.

Hundreds of miles away back in Horwich, Mrs Spencer had just taken delivery of that morning's *Horwich Chronicle*. She read with glee the article written by their new reporter, Samantha Spalding, about the new surgery which had attracted so much attention and, for a change, it was all positive. She looked down at Tiddles who was winding himself around her legs. She looked through the window at Billy the dumper truck driver who passed her door many times in a day. As always, he obeyed the "Dead Slow! 5 mph." imperative and waved cheerfully at her as he did so. She reached for the scissors. "Look, Tiddles, this is another article to go with our collection. I'll be running out of space soon and look this one mentions me and our new friends." Tiddles, looked up, meowed a little as she cut out the article carefully and moved to her front room.

Back in Heathrow and in the *First* cabin, the Jumbo was making final checks ready to depart.

Melissa brought two glasses of Laurent Perrier champagne and some heated nuts, sensing that the conversation in progress between them had been resolved; nevertheless, she withdrew noiselessly after putting them within their reach. As she did so, the noise from the Rolls-Royce engines changed from a whine to a satisfying hum as on-board generators cut in and the Jumbo was pushed back from its stand.

He raised his glass. "To you, someone who is very, very special."

"Special or foolish? If it hadn't been for Matilda Spencer we would have just the roof over our head in Vancouver, maybe not even that."

"And, my love, we would be fine with that. And so would your Aunt."

"But Tom, it was so close."

"Close it was, but as Mrs Spencer said to you, it was about time someone did you a favour.

Since you won all that money, you have tirelessly helped everyone that you could, everyone with whom you came into contact. I think she was right, it was high time it was your turn."

"But we are wealthier now that when I started."

"And knowing you, my love, we will find ever more inventive ways of helping those who are in desperate need. Just as we promised, our work will go on."

"Are you not mad with me for risking absolutely everything?"

"Mad? How can I be mad with someone who has given me everything, and I don't mean money. I mean all the things that money cannot buy. Someone who took my miserable, lonely life and turned it round with one blink from those gorgeous eyes."

"You say the nicest things."

"And it's all true. It's part of my training for writing romantic cards." She smiled. "Oh, I think you are going to be too busy to launch a new career," she advised with an enigmatic smile.

"Besides, *Petunia* isn't it time you went by your married name?"

"Don't you dare, Mr Plant! I'm going to change it by deed poll."

"You just love it."

"No I don't. I've been thinking of something else, how

about Poppy Pennine or Poppy Horwich?"

"No, can't see it. Sorry, it seems you're stuck with it. You'd miss it anyway."

"Well, it certainly isn't a name to give to a little plant."

For the moment her words didn't register and his conversation continued.

"Rich or poor, we go on and, as you said, the money isn't important; it just means we can help a few more along the way in England and Canada and wherever else we find them?"

"Just the two of us?"

"Well, I know it was a close run thing but you, sorry we, are 200 million richer."

"You know what this means don't you?"

"Go on?"

"We are going to be busier than ever, helping the disadvantaged and those down on their luck in England and in Canada and wherever else we encounter them. Well, perhaps not me so much, but certainly you…"

"Why just me, when helping others is your passion?"

"Always, always, but you wouldn't want," she looked down. He saw that she'd not touched her champagne, only her orange juice. Then, he finally registered what she had said. His mouth opened but no words came.

"wouldn't want a woman in my condition running round would you?" she patted her tummy.

"A little plant!" His eyes were now aglow as he kissed her lightly. "Have I time to go back and get another moose?"

"No, but I think a little toast to the three of us." She raised her glass of orange juice and their glasses clinked together.

"I love you, Poppy. Here's to new adventures."

Melissa rushed over. "Forgive me, but did I hear that congratulations are in order?" Poppy nodded. "I just knew! I am so pleased for the two of you."

Poppy pushed the glass of champagne to him – "the three of us," she said as she patted her tummy, once again.

He heard the engines scream as Melissa departed quickly to strap herself in. The Jumbo began to accelerate as the noise came to a crescendo and the plane leapt forwards as the brakes were released.

"So, there's no time to get another moose then?"

"No, I think you'd better just shut up and kiss me. Besides, I think we'll have lots of time for soft toys and so much more. I love you, Tom."

"Thank you, Poppy..." He began tantalisingly, then paused, his eyes aglow.

"Don't you dare say it," she pressed his lips with her finger.

"Can't help it. Thank you for filling my life with so many things that money just cannot buy. I love you too. I love you, Poppy Plant."

"That's it! I knew you couldn't resist it. I am definitely going to change it and if we have a girl there's no way we are going to call her Lavender, or Heath if it's a boy."

"Agreed! Here's to new adventures."

She smiled as their glasses clinked again.

The sparkle returned in those eyes of a limitless blue that shamed the bright sky towards which the Jumbo jet climbed as it clawed skyward and set a course to meet up with another brilliant blue dawn that awaited them in Vancouver.

She kissed him again and again.

THE END